Outside
Is the
Ocean

Mt. Lebanon Public Library
16 Castle Shannon Blvd.
Pittsburgh, PA 15228-2252
412-531-1912
www.mtlebanonlibrary.org
11/2017

The

Iowa

Short

Fiction

Award

In honor of

James O. Freedman

University

of Iowa Press

Iowa City

*Matthew
Lansburgh*

*Outside
Is the
Ocean*

University of Iowa Press, Iowa City 52242

Copyright © 2017 by Matthew Lansburgh

www.uipress.uiowa.edu

Printed in the United States of America

The University of Iowa Press is a member of Green Press
Initiative and is committed to preserving natural resources.
Printed on acid-free paper

Library of Congress Cataloging-in-Publication Data

Names: Lansburgh, Matthew, author.

Title: Outside is the ocean / Matthew Lansburgh.

Description: Iowa City : University Of Iowa Press, 2017. |
Series: Iowa Short Fiction Award

Identifiers: LCCN 2017005969 | ISBN 978-1-60938-527-9 (pbk) |
ISBN 978-1-60938-528-6 (ebk)

Subjects: | BISAC: FICTION / Short Stories (single author).

Classification: LCC PS3612.A5858 A6 2017 | DDC 813/.6—dc23

LC record available at https://lccn.loc.gov/2017005969

For my mother and for Stan

Contents

ACKNOWLEDGMENTS

This book would not exist without the support, encouragement, and insight I've received from more people than I can adequately acknowledge here.

I would like to thank the University of Iowa Press and Andre Dubus III as well as the editors of the journals that first published many of the stories in this collection: "Outside Is the Ocean" in *Ecotone* (2017); a modified version of "Enormous in the Moonlight" and "Buddy" in *Glimmer Train* (2017); "The Lure" in *The Florida Review* (2016); "Driving North" in *Michigan Quarterly Review* (2016); "The Sky and the Night" in *Joyland* (2016); "Queen of Sheba" in *Cosmonauts Avenue* (2015); "Gunpoint" in *Columbia: A Journal of Literature & Art* (2014); "House Made of Snow" in *Slice* (2011); and "California" in *Slice* (2010). I am also grateful to Francisco Goldman for selecting "Gunpoint" as the winner of *Columbia*'s 2013 fiction contest and to Lisa Roney for selecting "The Lure" as the winner of *The Florida Review*'s 2015 fiction contest.

In addition, I am indebted to the teachers and mentors whose encouragement and thoughtful feedback have helped me grow as a writer over the past many years. This list is long and includes not just the professors with whom I studied at NYU's MFA Program in Creative Writing—especially, Jonathan Safran Foer, Zadie Smith, Darin Strauss, David Lipsky, Hannah Tinti, and Amy Hempel—but also Lori Ostlund, Paul LaFarge, Paul Yoon, Anna Solomon, Josh Weil, David Leavitt, Mark Wisniewski, and Will Allison.

Finally, I would like to thank my family, above all, my parents, for encouraging me to write and pursue my true passion: thank you for being open-minded and courageous. And my close friends who read many drafts of these stories, and who kept me going through thick and thin.

And, of course, Stan: purveyor of everything good and worthwhile and necessary—smart, thoughtful feedback on page after page and draft after draft; encouragement and support, day in and day out; patience; and most importantly love.

Outside
Is the
Ocean

1993

Queen
of
Sheba

Al gives me zero. All day long he sits glued to his armchair, drinking glass after glass of V8 juice and making a mess with his crackers. The crumbs end up everywhere—the upholstery and carpet, not to mention the little table he drags in front of the TV. At dinner, he's tight-lipped. In bed it's the same. For quite some time, he's been unable to satisfy me. From the moment we met, he had difficulty in this department. He was not even seventy then. I was just fifty-four. For a woman, especially one who keeps in good shape, this is quite young.

I play violin. I play tennis. I go hiking and skiing. None of this interests him. Finally, for my birthday, I said, "That's it! I go crazy with you. At least take me on a small trip." I called up his daughter, Laurie, who has this adorable little Crystal, and invited them along to Las Vegas. "Come on," I said, "we go to the Circus Circus hotel."

In summertime this place is a steal—$29.95 a night. For that you get everything: a huge amusement park full of games, including roller coaster, slot machines coming out of your ears, and of course the main attraction: a circus, complete with stadium seating.

All night I stayed up packing the car, making nice *jagdwurst* sandwiches and a wonderful curry from these frozen shrimp they sell by the package at Vons. I made sure to bring lemon-lime Hansens along and even a few M&Ms.

Laurie is just like her father—provides no help whatsoever. She showed up empty-handed, wearing these sweatpants of hers. "What's wrong?" I said. "Aren't you happy to go on vacation?"

"Yeah. We're happy." She works as a nurse at the hospital and always shuffles behind. Crystal at least shows her enthusiasm. She brought along two dolls in nice outfits and these picture books I bought her for Christmas full of beautiful castles from Füssen and Heidelberg and the Swabian Alps.

Last year, Laurie's husband had an affair with a woman from church. Laurie came home at lunch and found them in bed. For three months she cried. "Laurie," I told her, "these things happen sometimes. You must learn to forgive."

No, no, no. She wouldn't listen. She went to a lawyer for a divorce. "Don't be so rash," I said. "Raising a child on one's own isn't that easy."

"How can I ever trust him again?" she asked me, blowing her nose. "What kind of example would that be for Crystal?"

What could I say? Was I going to tell her that Al himself had once cheated on me? Some people are too stubborn to listen. Laurie is still young. She thinks the world will hand her French toast on a silver platter. She didn't grow up in wartime when a pair of shoes was a luxury not to be had. She never struggled on food stamps. Look at me, I wanted to tell her. Do you think your father is the Prince Charming I had in mind? We all make compromises in life.

Six hours we drove, Al at the wheel. Luckily, this is one area where he can deliver. Never gets tired. Crystal behaved herself nicely in the backseat while I taught her the songs I myself sang as a girl in Germany. Laurie said nothing, watching us with a long face.

Finally we arrived. The hotel was fantastic: super luxurious. "Come on, Crystal," I said. "Let's have ourselves some fun!" We rushed down to the nickel machines before even checking into the room. Crystal held on to the cup with the coins and kept count. First try, I hit three cherries—twenty-dollar payout came down. Twenty bucks! I put half in my purse and kept going.

Few minutes later there came this man with a very thin moustache, like an inspector. "Madam," he said, "minors are not permitted in the casino."

"She just sits here politely and watches. I don't allow her to play."

"Sorry, ma'am. House rules. No one allowed under twenty-one."

"That's ridiculous. We drove all the way from California to give her some fun. Today is her birthday!"

"No exceptions," he said, very stern.

"Fine. Upstairs with Papa," I instructed. "It's time for the old guy to carry his weight."

That night Al took us for a fabulous all-you-can-eat dinner, though as usual, he refused to wear decent clothes—he insisted on this old red shirt he always has on, while I put on my gorgeous burgundy outfit. Very sexy. The men in line couldn't take their eyes off me.

The meal was out of this world. Crystal loaded up on the sweet tangerines she adores, while Al and I gorged ourselves on salmon filets and expensive prime rib. Laurie sat there with a small salad. "Come on," I said, "have yourself some of these entrees. It all comes included."

"I'm on a diet," she responded. She's always on a diet. Doesn't do any good. I have offered many times to teach her tennis, but she never accepts.

"Fine, but if you want a nice body, you need to get out of the house. You can't just sit in front of the TV eating powdered donuts out of the box."

"Don't tell me what to do," she said, very snippy. "My weight issues are my business, not yours."

"Suit yourself. Just don't expect room service later tonight."

After the meal, Al wanted to go back to the room. No big surprise. Laurie and Crystal went with him to watch TV while I strolled around on my own. Immediately a wonderfully dressed gentleman with blazer and tie caught my eye. He was busy teaching a card game to a group of old fogies, and as I approached he looked up and gave me a movie-star smile. "Why don't you join us," he said, pointing to the last empty seat. I sat down very student-like while he continued his spiel. Blackjack was the name. For me it was new. You strive to get twenty-one but no more. He spoke in a baritone voice.

"There is such a thing as a hard sixteen and a soft sixteen," he explained, looking into my eyes. "The ace can be played two ways, aces and eights should always be split. Then there is also insurance. At seventeen the house stands."

Luckily I had paper and pen in my handbag so I could write it all down.

Next he wanted us to pull out our money. "Ha! Not a chance! I watch but don't play."

"Come on," he said. "Just give it a try."

"Fine, I buy two chips with my afternoon winnings." So I gave my ten-dollar bill, and he dealt out the cards. First hand, I lost five smackers.

"That's it," I said. "I take my chip and go home."

"Go home? You just got here."

He had this very persuasive way.

"No, no, no." Off I went to the ladies' room.

When I came out, who did I see but the same gentleman. He came over to me, very suave. "You're a knockout. What's a beautiful woman like you doing here all alone?"

"I came here with a girlfriend of mine who's sick with the flu. She's upstairs in her nightie."

"Come, let me buy you a drink." He had ocean blue eyes and thick silver hair.

"A drink would be wonderful. I love a cold Coke."

He put out his arm and escorted me through the halls. "A Coke for the lady and a Bloody Mary for me," he told the bartender.

Then he turned to me and, just like that, he kissed my hand. "You're a beautiful woman," he confided, caressing my skin.

I almost collapsed to the floor.

"Where do you come from?"

"Me? From Bavaria. Near the Austrian border."

"Ah, Bavaria. Can you yodel?"

"Of course, but not here."

Then he tried to entice me back to his place. Joops! I got up. "I have to go," I said. "My friend is in need. She's sick as a dog, and I promised to bring her some soup."

"So quickly? We're just getting acquainted."

He rubbed his finger over my arm, then gave me the most sensual kiss. Right there at the bar. Luckily, my gang was nowhere around. Down the hall I went, rather coquettishly, leaving my name on a slip of white paper.

All night, I was unable to sleep. For two years I had been a good girl, respecting my vows. Even when I found out about Al and Gloria Delgado, I still didn't stray. "I forgive you," I told him, when he came crying to me, saying he'd made a mistake. Then, six months ago, he had a stroke and I also stuck by. "It's okay," I said. "I'll help you recover." I drove him to physical therapy and made hand exercises to help him regain his strength. A woman should stick by her man, I told myself. After all, women my age don't have that many options. Elke, my friend from the German club, tells me I'm lucky to have someone like Al. "At least he takes you to dinner," she says. "The only men who ever call me split everything right down the middle."

Eventually the sun peeked into our room, and I put on my house shoes. I wanted to go down the hall to retrieve ice cubes from the machine, but when I opened the door, what did I see before me but an oversized bouquet of red roses. I thought it must be a mistake. They have delivered these flowers to the wrong room. I bent down to look at the card and saw "To Heike" printed on the envelope. "You've stolen my heart," was written inside. "Meet me tonight at the bar for a drink. I get off at 9:00. Your admirer, Jerome."

What on earth can I do with these flowers? I wondered. Quickly, I took them into the bathroom. Each flower was gorgeous—very long-stemmed. Must have cost him a fortune!

My God, I said to myself. This is a true gentleman.

I sat in the bathroom for a good twenty minutes trying to figure out what possibly to tell Al. Should I say the flowers came from my son in Boston? From this student who comes over on Tuesdays to learn violin? It had been years since Al gave me a bouquet. Finally, he got up and knocked at the bathroom.

"You never guess who sent me some roses," I said. "Bernie Kramer." Bernie is my tennis date each Wednesday at 10:00. Al knows I don't find him one bit attractive; I call him the shrimp, he's so short.

"Bernie? Bernie sent you red roses?"

"Yes, you know how he has this little crush on me. He wanted to do something nice for my birthday."

"Oh," said Al, sitting down on the pot. "You told him you were going to Vegas?"

"Of course I told him. I had to cancel our tennis. Are you jealous?"

"Of the shrimp? Should I be?"

"Come on," I said, "I invite you all to breakfast." I rounded up the gang and went downstairs where they had this wonderful buffet. Ninety-nine cents apiece. We loaded up on thick sausages, French toast, and sunny-side eggs. In went a few of the links into my handbag, wrapped in napkins, so we would have something to eat later on. I had promised Crystal we go to the water slide, and everyone knows how expensive the lunches there are.

After brushing our teeth, off we went to Soak City. We found a parking spot in the shade, and Laurie and Al insisted on waiting for us under an elm.

"Come on, Laurie," I said, "put on your bikini. It'll be fun!"

Of course she had no interest in accompanying us.

"Why not? Didn't you bring it along?"

"No, Heike," she said to me, very haughty. "I did not bring my bikini along."

Crystal had on her cute butterfly one-piece that I bought her last summer. She really is adorable, so full of life with her rosy cheeks and blond hair.

"I'll race you, Grandma," she said, chasing up the hill and getting in line. First run, we went on one mat together, splashing into the water full force. The speed you pick up going down these long tubes is incredible! Immediately, the girl raced back up to the top. All afternoon, we had a ball. It's good for the child to have fun, I thought to myself. Tonight will be my turn. I wanted to tire her out so she'd fall asleep.

Sure enough, by 9:30, Crystal and Laurie were snoring up a storm next door in their room. Al had on his pajamas and was watching a show discussing black monkeys who live in the snow.

"You know what," I said, "I think I go down and play a few more slot machines. For some reason, I have excess energy."

"Now?"

"Yep. Make yourself comfy. I'll be back later on."

Quickly I changed into my nice low-cut dress and gave him a kiss on the cheek. The Queen of Sheba could come out in the nude and he'd give no reaction at all.

The walk alone to the bar was quite something. I felt like royalty, making my way through these corridors, each one with wall-to-wall carpet. Everywhere you enjoy shiny brass.

I arrived at the bar, and sure enough Jerome was waiting in a wonderful cream-colored suit, sipping something delicious.

"You look ravishing," he said to me.

"Do I?"

I stood there for a moment, letting him soak it all in.

"I've been hoping you'd show up," he said. Immediately, he called the bartender over. "Louie, bring this beautiful woman your best strawberry margarita."

"A strawberry margarita? Are you trying to get me drunk right away?"

"Would you prefer something else?"

"No, no, a strawberry margarita sounds fabulous. I haven't had one in years."

Well, now here's a refined gentleman, I thought to myself. How on earth am I going to entertain him? So I told him these stories about my mother's family in Leipzig before the war and how they sold furs and went to the opera. I narrated the struggles I had as a single mother until I met Gerry, my knight in polished armor.

Jerome took quite an interest, listening very well, then said, "Heike, come with me for a walk. I know a place in the desert where at night the moon lights up all the cactus. It's very romantic. I want to share it with you."

"A walk? At such a late hour?"

"Come on," he said.

What is there really to lose? I thought. A man this age surely won't kidnap me. All year I sit at home, night after night. Why not live a little?

"Fine. I accompany you. But promise me I return before midnight. We leave tomorrow at eight in the morning, and I don't want my friend to worry so much."

"We'll be back in time. The night is still young."

So we started out to his car and he guided me along, holding my arm in his hand. Just feeling him next to me made my legs tingle. Sure enough, he drove a Cadillac—very big and fancy with thick cushions. He put his key into the ignition and made some nice music. Then he turned to me and said, "I'm crazy for you, you know that? You're all I've been thinking about."

"My goodness," I said.

"Shhh. No talking." He leaned over, took me into his arms, and gave me a kiss. A real kiss. So passionate I almost passed out. He put his hands through my hair and his lips on my neck. I can still smell his cologne.

"You have perfect breasts," he said to me. "So many other women get implants nowadays. Yours are so natural."

"Of course they're natural. I come from the Alps!"

Then he got very fresh.

"Jerome," I said. "What are you doing?"

"I crave you, Heike."

"What about this wonderful walk you promised?"

"The walk? Do you want me to stop?"

"Yes, I'm not this kind of woman." He seemed rather surprised, but he straightened himself.

"I'm sorry. I got carried away. I hope you'll forgive me."

"Of course I forgive you," I said, wondering whether I was too firm in my rejection of him.

Jerome drove me through the Las Vegas strip full of neon lights, giving me a detailed tour. "Here's the famous Bellagio where they have paintings by Renoir and van Gogh." Then he pointed out the Sphinx, and I wondered whether he might reach over to hold my hand. I had a feeling that once we arrived at these cactus, he would try to seduce me again.

Eventually we left the city and began driving out through the desert. "I wish you didn't live so far away," he said to me. "I feel a real connection to you." He told me how lonely he had been since his wife passed away. For the past three years, he lived like a monk.

"I know what you mean. It's hard living alone."

Few minutes later, he pulled to the side of the road. "This is it?" I asked.

"Don't sound so disappointed. You'll see how special it is." We got out of the car and looked up at the sky; everywhere there were stars, tiny but vivid. There, in the distance, was the moon keeping watch. "Do you see the Little Dipper?" he asked. He pointed out the handle with the North Star. I wondered whether he would try to embrace me again. I closed my eyes, allowing him to come close.

"See there, down this path," he said, "there are some of the largest boulders in the state of Nevada."

"Is that so?" I said, looking at him. He took my hand in his and led me down a small path. Luckily, my shoes had flat soles. He told me this was where he went when he wanted to be alone and feel connected to nature. "Helen and I came here on our wedding night. We camped over there, right under the stars."

We walked together until the path became too narrow for us to go side by side, and I couldn't help but think about Gerry. Once, before he got cancer, we went down to the beach with a flashlight. We packed a blanket and a bottle of wine and made love in front of the waves. I wondered whether Gerry could see me from Heaven, amidst these large rocks, and I wished I was walking with him. Even at the end when he was nearly unable to move, he told me he loved me and kissed me goodnight.

"Jerome, I have something to tell you," I said finally. "I hope you will not think less of me. I am actually married. I live with a man in California." I apologized for lying to him.

"Really?" he said, stopping near one of the cactus. "But you don't have a ring."

The moon was high, and it made the rocks and cactus look almost silver. In this empty desert, everything seemed far away. Then, for some reason, I began to cry. "Jerome, would you mind holding me?"

He complied, embracing me nicely. I told him that after Gerry died, I didn't know whether I would ever find someone to be with again. I told him about my sleepless nights alone in the house and about Al. "He's a nice man," I said. "He swims in the pool every day. He used to before he had the stroke. Now, his shoulder bothers him all the time. The doctors say it may never get better. At first I thought he loved me, but then I found out he made love to a checker at Vons. He told me she seduced him, but it doesn't matter."

I stopped for a moment and went over to one of the rocks to sit down. "Need a hankie?" Jerome asked, handing me his kerchief.

I told him about Laurie, how much she hates me. "I try to be nice to her. I used to pick her little girl up from school sometimes, but now she forbids me to do even this. She tells me it's all taken care of. She says she's a Christian, but she can be terribly cold. I was hoping so much we could be a nice family, but last Christmas she didn't even want to come over. She just dropped the presents off at the door and said they were late for a shindig at church."

Jerome told me he was sorry and put his hand on my back.

"Jerome," I said, looking at him. "Do you think I'm still pretty?"

"Of course, Heike. You're a very beautiful woman. You know that."

"But I have so many wrinkles. It must be from too much tennis. After Gerry died, I got a facelift, but that was a disaster. The doctor was a butcher. For months my skin was all swollen and red."

"You don't need any facelifts. You're very attractive. Look, it's getting late. We should probably be heading back. Are you okay? Can you walk?"

"Yes, I'm fine. I'm sorry. I shouldn't have spilled all these beans."

At first, as we retraced our steps, he put his arm around me, but then, where the path became narrow, he walked in front once again. The closer we got to the car, the more I wished I hadn't been so honest with him. *You should have just kept your mouth shut,* I told myself. *Now your makeup is ruined.*

"I think I got a blister," I said when we arrived to his Cadillac. "Do you mind if I take off my shoe?" Sure enough, the skin on my heel was starting to bleed. He offered me a Band-Aid and then, as he started the engine, I smoothed down the fabric of my red dress, accentuating the length of my legs.

"Be honest," I said. "Do you think it's possible to find love at our age? Do you think you will ever find it again?"

He leaned forward and turned on the radio. "Love is a hard thing. Some people never find it at all."

From the speakers came music like they present in old movies. It reminded me of a record Gerry played for me when we first met. "This is nice," I said.

"Yeah, I'm just not in the mood," he replied, turning the knob until a man's voice came into the car. The man talked about news from the Orient, how villagers capture dogs and sell them for fur.

The sky was black, and as we drove, Jerome kept very quiet. "Tell me about Helen," I eventually said.

"Helen? What do you mean?"

"What was she like?"

"We met in high school. She was the smartest girl in our class. What can I say? I was lucky to have her for as long as I did." He rolled down his window and kept both hands on the wheel. Suddenly, I felt quite sad. We stopped at a red light not far from the hotel. "Have you thought of getting remarried?" I finally asked.

"Me? I'm too old for that now."

"You're not too old. You still have the golden years to enjoy."

He smiled but kept his eyes on the road, without changing direction.

We pulled into the entrance of the Circus Circus, and he drove me up to the door. "Here you go, Heike. I hope your friend's feeling better."

I looked at him and wondered whether he would turn off the motor. "That's it?" I said.

"Yep, that's it. It's late. I need to get home."

"Don't you at least want my address?" I got out a pen so we could exchange information. "Ventana Beach is very nice," I told him. "Perhaps one day you can come visit."

He smiled at me, but the smile was cold—like a businessman writing a check. I leaned forward and gave him a kiss on the cheek, then got out of the car. Inside the hotel, the slot machines were still wide-awake. I walked through the lobby and wondered what the future would hold. Tomorrow we would drive back to Ventana Beach and that would be that.

At the elevator, I looked at myself in the mirror—I put on more lipstick and fixed up my hair, in case Al had trouble sleeping. Sometimes, at home, I stay up watching TV, and when I get into bed, Al has not yet fallen asleep. Even if he cannot make love, he still likes to embrace.

When I opened the door to the room, I saw that Al had left the bathroom light on for me. I saw him lying in bed, under the covers. "Al?" I called, softly. I stood in the hallway, next to the closet, letting my eyes adjust.

I put on my nightgown and got into bed, replaying the night in my head. You always say the wrong thing, I scolded myself. You ruined everything. You should have just kept your mouth shut and had a good time. Something about the sheets and my pillow smelled smoky and gray. Then, out from the darkness, Al reached over and touched my arm. "Did you make us rich?" he asked.

"What?"

"Did you hit the jackpot?"

"Did I wake you up, darling?"

"Nah, I've been awake. I couldn't sleep. The damn ice machine down the hall keeps making a racket."

"You better get some rest," I told him, knowing I shouldn't say more. "Tomorrow is a long drive."

"I'll be okay. Tell me, honey, did you have a good birthday?"

I lay there for a minute, looking up at the ceiling, wishing for some kind of sound. Through the curtains, a light from the parking lot shined in from outside. Maybe Elke is right, I thought to myself. A bird in one's hand gives more eggs than a flock in the bush. "It was one of my best," I said to him then.

1967
California

Heike wonders whether she's made a mistake. She opens her handbag and examines a small piece of paper— TWA 302 11:23—then looks at the sign near the doorway where, until a few moments ago, passengers from her husband's plane were still disembarking. Around her, people embrace one another, some with tears in their eyes.

"Everything is fine, *mein Schatz*," she tells Stewart, who sits in his stroller, wearing corduroy pants and a shirt folded once at the sleeves. "Daddy is getting his things. He must have been late to the airport and was forced to sit at the back of the plane." But even as Heike formulates these sentences, she knows her explanation is unlikely. Raymond is not at the back of the plane. Raymond would have come down the walkway quickly, a bag in each hand. Could it be that she wrote down the wrong flight number?

Four nights ago, when the phone rang, it was half past one in the morning, and Heike fumbled with the receiver. "What's going on over there?" Raymond asked, and she apologized as she tried to turn on the light. Her husband was calling from England, where he'd spent the past seven weeks doing research for a book on illuminated manuscripts. For days she'd hoped to receive a card or a letter. She sat near the phone each afternoon, when Stewart was taking his nap, willing it to ring. The call lasted three minutes at most. It was dark outside, and the bedroom was cold, and there was a bit of static on the line. Raymond told her his return would be delayed by two days, and then, before he hung up, he said something she did not understand. The word—or was it a phrase?—had a strong *r* sound, something with an *r* and a *b* or maybe a *v*.

Heike did not return the receiver to the cradle right away. The sound of the dial tone was strangely comforting, and, sitting on the edge of the bed, she imagined the voice of a friend. In California, before she'd moved to this town in the Rockies, Heike had rented a room from an elderly woman named Sylvia who liked to make large pots of soup with turnips and other root vegetables. Sometimes Heike thought about calling her on the phone. What would Heike say? Would she tell Sylvia the truth? *My husband is going to leave me. I can tell by the way he flirts in front of my eyes. By the way he refuses to touch me.*

Heike had seen Raymond meet a woman at a party last spring. The woman was poised and refined, and Raymond had walked across the room to get her a drink. Everything about her was perfect, even her name. Heike had studied the woman, Miss Elizabeth Brown, had watched her laugh at Raymond's jokes, had envied her movie-star teeth. Of course that was the kind of person Raymond should be with. Heike told Raymond from the beginning that she herself was not right for him. She told him he should marry someone with a background like his, someone who had gone to college and had elegant taste.

"Don't be ridiculous," he said. "I love the fact that you grew up on a farm."

And for a time Heike believed him, though the place she lived as a girl was not a farm. "We lived in a hut near a large forest," she said on their first outing together. "There was no running water, but we had fat rabbits that we kept in a cage."

"I've always had a thing for German girls," he said when they first met. "I'll bet you look great in a dirndl." She was working as a teller at a bank, and, soon enough, her colleagues declared him smitten. Six times he brought chocolates and baskets of fruit.

"Mr. Winter, are you trying to get me into trouble?" she said, half joking with him. "If you are flirting with me and I make a mistake, they deduct the shortage from my paycheck." She counted out his withdrawal, and he told her she had beautiful hands. "Enough now. There are customers waiting patient behind you in line."

Perhaps, as she fumbled with the pen, as she pressed the dry tip into the piece of paper on the nightstand, she reversed two of the numbers. Heike is new to the world of airports and flights. Her only trip by plane was with Raymond himself, after their wedding, from Los Angeles to Chicago, where his family lived. She'd been nervous to get on the aircraft, nervous and excited—and, as the plane lifted off, she squeezed her new husband's hand. Their courtship had moved quickly. Night after night, he knocked on her door, bringing scarves and poems he'd written. "Come with me for a drive," he pleaded. "The moon is so beautiful." His fiancée had broken his heart, he confessed, and he couldn't stand being alone. On the third night they drove to the top of a mountain, overlooking the beach and the sea, where he told her the names of the stars. He brought her a bouquet of dried peonies with lavender and rose hips. She didn't ask why the flowers were dry.

"Excuse me, ma'am," she says to a woman in a uniform here at the gate. "Would you be so kind and tell me whether there are any more passengers still leaving the aircraft?"

The woman turns out to be friendly. She tells Heike the plane is empty, but she offers to see whether Raymond was booked on the flight. The woman's name is Michelle, a nice name, the kind of name Heike would have chosen for Stewart if he'd been a girl. She has makeup that is tastefully applied and a bosom that doesn't call attention to itself. She peppers Heike with questions: Did Raymond spend the night in New York before catching his flight back to Denver? Could he have missed a connection and boarded a later flight? What was the name of the hotel where he'd stayed?

These are the things Heike herself should have asked. It would have been natural for a wife to ask her husband whether he would spend the night in New York before returning home. The plane from London to New York would have arrived in the late afternoon, and Raymond might not have been able to catch a flight to Denver until the next day. As Michelle turns to walk away, Heike wants to say something else. For a moment she wonders whether she should follow Michelle. Perhaps she would take pity on Heike. "Come home with me," she might say. "You and your son can spend the night in our house."

Heike stays where she is. In the distance, she thinks she can see Raymond now. A man, about Raymond's height, in a blazer, is walking next to a woman. Could this be the same woman he met at the party in April? A professor from Raymond's department was retiring, and Raymond had put on his tweed suit. Heike remembers standing in front of a painting of a lighthouse surrounded by lashing waves while Raymond talked to the woman, a librarian from England who'd come to Colorado to give lectures on Renaissance art.

"Elizabeth was really something," he said on their way home. "Did you think she was striking?" Heike remembers feeling confused by the question, confused and almost ashamed.

"Striking?" she asked. "What means striking? Is she the mother of your child? Did she bear you a son?" She wonders how someone like Michelle would have reacted.

"Yes, Heike, she bore me a child. Didn't you see her there with my children? They were wearing little yellow outfits and had teddy bears. Weren't they cute?"

Stewart must be getting hungry now, Heike thinks. Soon it will be time for his nap. She observes the couple, and then, before she is certain, she surprises herself. She turns and walks away, pushing the stroller toward the long corridor with polished white floors.

Driving home, she comes up with a plan. It is still early enough for her to pack up their things and stop at the bank. There are two suitcases in the basement she can use. They wouldn't need much—just their clothes, her violin, and a few of Stewart's stuffed animals. They can leave while it is still light, drive west to Grand Junction, and spend the night in a hotel. Tomorrow, at sunrise, they can continue on to Cedar City. Heike wonders how many days it would take them to reach Ventana Beach. Four years ago, the drive from California took just two and a half days, though Raymond sped the whole way. They'd been married ten weeks when he accepted the job, telling her she should be proud.

By the time she pulls into the driveway, however, Heike's plans have already begun to fray. Even if she took everything out of the household account, it wouldn't be enough to make a new life. She tells herself that it must have been the day of Raymond's return she misunderstood. His flight must be arriving tomorrow. The mistake is actually good luck, she decides. She was rushed getting ready this morning and the outfit she chose is not becoming on her.

The sky has been overcast for nearly a week, but after lunch the sun breaks through the clouds. "What shall we do, *mein Liebchen?*" she asks Stewart, who is playing with a fuzzel from his favorite green blanket. "Do you want to go to the pond with *Mutti* and make the duckies a little bit happy?" And when he nods yes, she smiles and puts her hand on his cheek. "We bring them some bread crumbs," she says, taking heels of dark rye from beneath the sink. Even in deepest winter, she goes on walks with her son—bundles him up and pushes him down Warburt Lane and Beatrice Avenue and other streets whose names she's learned to pronounce. Now and then she sees a familiar face, the wife of another professor or an elderly gentleman sweeping his porch, though she rarely does more than wave. In school, English was always her best subject, but here in America people talk quickly and sometimes—often—she still makes mistakes. Raymond likes to correct her. "Adverbs end in *l-y*," he instructs.

All summer long she's used her savings to pay the girl down the street, a high school student, to tutor her. "Even if it is a small thing, please correct me. It is very important that I make not so many grammatical errors." She meets the girl three times a week. Yesterday they were practicing the past perfect tense: *On Tuesday Eloise ate baked potatoes, but last week she had eaten nothing but ham.*

Occasionally, on mornings when Heike feels more certain, she stops by the bakery and asks the man with the heavy beard whether he has any bread she can feed to the birds at the lake, the mother and her little duckies. Even to him, she calls them her duckies, and he smiles and hands her a loaf. Heike zips Stewart's coat up to his chin. She ties off the bag of scraps she's collected and tucks it into her pocket. Today she won't stop at the baker's. She turned thirty only recently, but already she feels she has made mistakes that cannot be undone.

Heike maneuvers the stroller onto the sidewalk and heads past the angular hedges and lawns. The air is crisp. When she was a girl, her mother took her up to the mountains on this kind of day to pick berries that were blue and black and bright red. They each carried a basket, and her mother taught her songs from the *Gewandhaus* choir.

At the lake, the ducks know that Heike and Stewart have brought something for them. Even before she's untied the bag, they begin greeting her. Stewart's hands are too small to break the bread into pieces, so Heike helps, handing him bite-size chunks. "Be a big boy and throw it as far as you can," she says. "Make sure the little ones get a bit too. They're also hungry."

In California, in September, people are still wearing shorts. As a girl, she spent so many nights imagining what it would be like to walk without shoes on the sand. She saw photos in magazines of long strips of coast, with girls in bikinis and boys driving open-air cars, and she promised herself that when she was older she would move to America. "In California," she wrote to her mother, "it is always sunny and nice." She bought a postcard with palm trees, and she made a point of showing off the English she'd learned.

In the distance, Heike sees a woman walking, at the edge of the water, arm in arm with a man. The man stops and picks up a leaf from the ground. Soon, for a few short weeks, trees everywhere will light up the mountains with colors like pumpkins and squash. The forests will take on brilliant hues, and then, suddenly, everything will change and the leaves will fall to the ground. Heike imagines Elizabeth Brown's scarf in the wind—Raymond kissing her on the lips. She imagines him touching her hair. Her hair will have been touched by his hand.

Eventually, Heike's legs grow heavy, her hands cold. She picks up her pace and pushes the stroller back home, along the sidewalks of tree-lined streets with houses where mothers peel carrots and put scalloped potatoes and green bean casseroles into hot ovens. Heike envies these women—women whose friends stop by, unannounced, for coffee and cake, whose children play in the backyard while their parents sit together reading the paper. Occasionally, she sees these women at the grocery store, standing near the bins of apples, exchanging gossip and recipes, and she thinks about reaching over to touch one of them and solicit advice.

Perhaps Raymond did not go away to meet this Elizabeth Brown. Perhaps he flew to London simply to photograph manuscripts for the book he is writing. Why be so suspicious? She is silly, letting her thoughts run away. Tomorrow Raymond will return and everything will be fine.

That night, after she puts Stewart to bed, Heike sits on the couch to watch some TV. Before Raymond left, he adjusted the antennas, but now when she turns on the television, most of the stations come in full of static. The only channel that works has a show about the dog Lassie and her family. Heike has seen the program a few times and likes it. She finds it incredible how well-trained the collie is and what a good companion she makes. Tonight Timmy dresses Lassie up as a swami so she can tell the fortunes of children.

When the show ends, Heike turns off the lights and heads back upstairs. In bed, she can't fall asleep. Across the ocean, in Europe, it is almost certainly morning.

Even before the sun has fully awakened, Heike is out of the bed, turning on the bathroom heater. She takes off her nightgown and looks at herself in the mirror. She *regards* herself. This is a term she learned recently from the book she is reading, a book in which the heroine has long blond hair and blue eyes and a mole, like Marilyn Monroe. The heroine *regarded* herself in the mirror of her dressing room. She looks at her reflection—her torso, her breasts, her hips and legs—a woman in a bathroom with cold tile floors and window panes that distort the garden below.

Her hair is not blond; it is red. She has thick wiry hair that she has hated since she was a girl. *Dickes und widerspenstiges Haar,* her mother always said. Too thick and unruly. Her hair is red and her eyes are brown, not blue or hazel or green. She has freckles and a slight overbite. Of course Raymond has grown tired of her. What man would want to be married to a woman with an overbite and hair like that girl from Sweden with the monkey?

A clear sky is a good sign, she thinks, as she stands at the closet, examining the selection before her. She chooses something in gray—the wool suit Raymond bought her three months after their first lunch together. "She needs to look dignified," he told the attendants at the boutique, and at first she was flattered by the attention: women showing her fabrics, helping her try on pant-suits brought out on nice hangers. She'd never been to a store with couches and beautiful mirrors.

Heike powders her face and outlines her lips, applying the eye shadow recommended to her and the mascara that costs seventy-nine cents per slender tube. She puts her hair up in a bun. Yesterday was just a misunderstanding, she tells herself. Instead of Wednesday, Raymond must have said Thursday. Yesterday was her dress rehearsal, and today she is ready. She leaves herself plenty of time.

At the airport, Stewart sits in his stroller wearing a tan sweater, his hair nicely combed to the side. His mother stands beside him, watching the people step off the plane. Men in suits, carrying briefcases, women in high heels and hats. Heike is glad she and her son are dressed well; Raymond will see them and not be embarrassed. He will come down the corridor, in his long coat, with his leather satchel, and he will see his family waiting for him. She will embrace him and ask how his flight was. She will tell him that she and Stewart missed him and made him a pie. She arranges the words in her head, practicing the rules she has learned.

1976

Gunpoint

The summer before I started seventh grade, not long after Patty Hearst was sentenced to thirty-five years in prison, my mother married a man who owned a ranch house with a yard full of lemon trees. As far as she was concerned, she'd hit the jackpot. Gerry didn't drink, he had a job, and, whenever we went out to eat, he always picked up the check. After dating a string of losers, after moving from apartment to apartment at least once a year for nearly a decade, my mother told me—three weeks into her new relationship—that, no matter what, we could not spit on the luck God had given to us. "This chance is once in a lifetime," she said.

My mother met Gerry on a ski trip organized by Amway. She put the vacation on her credit card and arranged for me to stay with a family that lived down the street. "Bingo," she announced on the phone, four days after she left. "I met someone perfect. He's a little tight-lipped and has a tummy, but he's an accountant, and he owns a condo in Mammoth." A few months later they got engaged and we moved from Ventana Beach down to L.A.

In retrospect I realize that Gerry had no idea what he was getting himself into. He liked routine, he hated conflict, and he wasn't used to dealing with difficult people.

My mother, who immigrated to the United States at the age of twenty to work as a maid, has always been the kind of person who doesn't take no for an answer. Within a week of our move, she'd butted heads with Gerry's neighbor Sandi Sarconi by borrowing her rake without asking permission. My mother happened to be using the rake just as Sandi drove down the street in her red BMW. The incident probably wouldn't have been a big deal if my mother had simply apologized, but she tried to justify herself, explaining that Gerry's rake was too rusty to work properly, then using the discussion as a way to horn in on Sandi's weekly doubles game with Carol Wallace, a woman who lived up the block, and two other women my mother had been wanting to meet.

It promptly became clear to everyone involved that Sandi and Carol did not like my mother's style—didn't like the fact that my mother cut her own hair instead of going to a salon; that she brought *wiener schnitzel*, rather than lasagna, to Carol's annual potluck; that she let Gerry's dog, Goldie, defecate in people's front yards. In September, Carol called just as we'd sat down to dinner.

"Why hello there," Gerry said when he picked up the phone. He was wearing the same thing he put on every night after he got home from the office: worn jeans and a flannel shirt. "Is that so? I see. That's unfortunate. Yes, of course, I'll have a talk with her."

My mother, who'd been telling Gerry a story about how the cashier at Vons had tried to overcharge her for a bag of oranges, was wiping up the gravy on her plate with her finger. She had a worried look on her face, a guilty look. I'd seen the expression plenty of times.

"Carol says Patti Schneider saw you laying out in their back-yard with your top off," Gerry said when he hung up.

"Really?"

"*Yes, really.* Did you go swimming in her pool, Heike?"

"I went for a quick dip. Is that such a crime? I tried to knock, but no one was home."

"She says she saw you lay out on the deck and take off your top."

"That's ridiculous," my mother said, getting up from the table and clearing the plates. "I simply pulled down the straps a bit. She's just jealous of my beautiful figure."

Gerry took off his glasses and studied them, as if he'd been socked in the face.

"Everyone hates me," my mother complained to him a few weeks later. "You have your job. Stewart goes to school. I have nothing. I need a good friend." My mother had made Gerry his favorite meal—meatloaf with spätzle and fried onions—and she had tears on her cheeks. Gerry wasn't stupid. Even before she made the request, he knew what she had in mind. She wanted him to let Sabine, a woman my mother had met at the German bakery in Hawthorne, move in with us. Sabine was from Munich, and, after being evicted from her apartment because she had too many cats, she'd recently moved to a motel that rented rooms by the week.

"No, Heike," Gerry said. "There's not enough room."

"Don't be such a stick in the mud. We can put a futon in your office. I saw one for sale at the Goodwill—only fifteen dollars, including delivery." Gerry stared at my mother, using his fingernails to pluck the stray hairs that grew from the edge of his ears. "Wait till you meet her. She has warm eyes and a kind smile. Your heart will go out to her."

After dinner, when Gerry still hadn't given in, my mother became semihysterical. "You don't know what it's like for me here! Sometimes I almost kill myself. Is that what you want? To come home and find your wife hanging from a rope?" I was in my room studying, but I could hear everything. It wasn't the first time I'd heard my mother trot out the suicide card.

"Enough!" Gerry shouted. I got up from my desk and looked through the crack between my door and the wall in time to see him storming off to the garage.

"Model airplanes," my mother yelled, still in tears. "My husband loves model airplanes more than his own wife!"

We drove to Inglewood to visit Sabine on a Saturday morning. My mother had gotten up early, made French toast, and put on the halter top she used to wear when she had to take her car in to get fixed.

"Do I really have to go?" I asked as I watched my mother put her plate on the carpet so Goldie could lick up the Mrs. Butterworth's. I hated the fact that my mother let the dog eat off our dishes, and I was convinced we'd end up with worms.

"*Have to go?* It'll be fun. Gerry takes us to Marie Callender's for lunch."

"But I have homework."

"Ach! Who does homework on Saturday? Come on now. Behave or you won't get any pie."

I reminded her that I didn't like pie and said something about the science fair project I needed to work on, and then, when I knew I was fighting a losing battle, I went to my room to change out of my pajamas. The truth is I hadn't wanted to stay home to study. I was hoping that Jason McFarland—a kid who'd moved into the house next to the Wallaces in June—might knock on our door. Jason and I weren't friends exactly, but sometimes he'd stop by to see whether I wanted to go out to the bushes behind our house and look at a stash of dirty magazines he'd stolen from his father. For some reason, Jason had decided that a place at the back of our yard, behind the lemon trees, was the perfect hiding spot for his dad's porn: three *Penthouse* magazines full of lurid photos of Amber Williams and Tonya Lee and Felicity Light and other women whose names I've forgotten, in poses that for many years I could recall with surprising clarity, including the one of Tonya next to a fire truck with a bare-chested man in suspenders who had hair leading down to his navel and biceps that looked like the gym teacher's.

The first few times Jason and I snuck out back, usually after school when my mother was running errands, Jason led the way. I watched, the branches of the lemon trees digging into my back, while he unearthed the mildewed treasures and flipped through their pages. Jason was in eighth grade, only a year ahead of me, but already his voice had changed and he boasted an Adam's apple. I remember leaning close to him, ostensibly to get a better look at the photos—so close that sometimes my arm grazed his shoulder or forearm or some other part of his body. I studied the blond hairs that had begun to sprout from his cheeks and his upper lip. I remember wondering whether he had a boner.

I stayed still, nervous that we might be caught or that Jason might notice me gazing at him. The dirt was damp and soft, and its earthy smell rose up to meet the scent of the lemons. I imagined my mother coming into the garden and calling out to us. "Stewart!" she yelled once, after getting home from a tennis game and not finding me in the house. "Are you here?" I heard her voice carry across the lawn and the hedges, through the thicket of branches, and I froze.

"Don't be such a fag," Jason said, while she was still outside in her yellow Fila skirt, shouting my name. "She's not gonna find us." His breath was warm and made my ear tingle.

Sabine's motel was even more rundown than I expected. It was on a busy intersection, and the office windows were covered in bars. The only parking space was next to a group of guys in tank tops sitting on their motorcycles, and before Gerry had gotten out of the car, one of them called my mother *baby* and made a loud kissing sound.

"How long is this going to take?" I asked.

"That's enough! Do you want to ruin the only friendship I have?"

I trailed my mother and Gerry—who walked on the edges of his feet, complaining that his arches hurt—across the parking lot, toward a room with a door that looked like someone had tried to pry the knob off. My mother knocked, and a tall woman in a skimpy robe answered. "Heike, *Liebchen*," she exclaimed. "You came after all. Careful the cats do not run outside."

When I reached out to shake Sabine's hand, she leaned forward and embraced me. "Heike, you didn't tell me Stewart was so handsome! I bet all the girls are chasing after him right and left. How wonderful to finally meet you, my little Prince Charming."

"Likewise," I said, trying to keep some distance between her chest and mine.

Sabine's room was small and reeked of urine; the curtains were drawn, and the only light came from a small lamp next to the bed. Two litter boxes covered the carpet next to the dresser, and neither looked like it had been emptied in days. At the foot of her nightstand sat a bowl of dried cat food and a dish of water with something bloated floating on the surface.

"My goodness," said Gerry, gesturing toward the cats. "Are they all yours?" Two of the creatures were up on the dresser, trying to climb into a box of full of papers.

"Yes, these are my babies," Sabine said. She stroked one on the back and grinned, exposing a set of teeth that were too large for her mouth.

"Aren't they cute?" asked my mother, as she picked up a white kitten and cradled it like an infant. "Feel how soft." Gerry put his hand out tentatively to stroke the cat's fur. "See, *mein Schatz.* Gerry takes a liking to you."

"They are my blessing," said Sabine. "Without my *Bübchen,* I would not know how to survive. I do not have such a nice family." Sabine looked at me and then, before I could pull away, she put her hand on my thigh. I felt the skin of her palm, cool and moist as a raw chicken cutlet. "My ex-husband, Rolf, and I tried to have a child for many years. We wanted a son." Her robe had come open a bit, and I glimpsed a terrifying expanse of white skin.

Gerry told Sabine that she lucked out finding a hotel that allowed pets.

"*Ja.* They do not mind *die Bübchen.* My old landlord was quite cruel. He continually nailed papers to my door demanding that I must move out of my house. I was a good renter. I paid him on time. I was clean, but he insisted I leave. I am sure it was because of the cats. Only in America would such a thing happen. Gerry, do you know if this kind of thing is legal to do?"

Gerry started to respond, but my mother interrupted. "Of course it's illegal. What one does in one's own home is no one else's business. How could he have objected to a few kittens? Does he also throw his wife out if she has twins?" My mother and Gerry sat in plastic chairs while I sat on the bed next to Sabine. The air was thick with dander, and my eyes were watering; I felt like I'd been locked in a bunker. I sneezed twice, insisted I was having an allergic reaction, and asked whether I could wait in the car.

"Fine, Mr. Party Pooper. Just don't get anything out of these vending machines. We eat lunch soon."

Outside, the Hells Angels were gone, but two teenage boys were now doing wheelies on their bikes. The boys looked like they were in high school, and they didn't have shirts on. I tried not to stare but found myself glancing furtively at them, partly out of fear that they might ride over and do something to hurt me, partly because any guy who'd already gone through puberty caught my eye. Their nipples were larger than mine, and I could see veins on their arms. I myself was a late bloomer, and the fact that I hadn't sprouted as much hair under my arms or around my crotch as other kids in the locker room caused me perpetual angst. I stood next to the car wondering whether I should go back to Sabine's room to ask for the keys. A minute later one of the guys shouted something in Spanish, and they both laughed. I stared at the fender of Gerry's Oldsmobile, afraid to look up. I tried to wedge my right foot under one of its tires, pushing the front of my shoe into the space between the rubber and the asphalt until my toes hurt. Then I heard what sounded like a pebble hit the windshield. I looked up and saw the bigger of the two kids throw something else in my direction as they sped away, shouting, *Maricón*.

My mother kept telling me I should be happy she married Gerry. She said that Gerry had saved us from being homeless, but Gerry wasn't the kind of father I'd hoped for. He didn't mess up my hair with the palm of his hand when we were standing in line at McDonald's or tickle me until my stomach hurt. He didn't take me Boogie Boarding in the summer. Most of the time, he just wanted to sit in his easy chair and be left alone.

Occasionally I wondered what it would feel like to be kidnapped. I imagined men wearing masks driving up in a van and forcing me inside at gunpoint. I pictured them pinning me to the floor and taping my mouth shut, sending my parents a ransom note like I'd seen on TV. I played out various scenarios in my head: my mother calling my father in Colorado, pleading with him to send money; my father flying in to meet the police, then driving around town with my mother, putting up posters with a photo of me; my parents standing next to each other in a house I'd never seen—a two-story house with a nice living room and a pool in the back—surrounded by men in FBI uniforms, wearing headphones and hovering over tape recorders they turned on each time the kidnappers called.

Over the next several days, as I lay in bed at night trying to fall asleep, I heard my mother and Gerry having more sex than usual. My room shared a wall with the master bedroom, and I often heard, if not their exact conversations, then at least the murmur of their voices, punctuated with my mother's occasional laughter and yelps. I knew what my mother was up to. She'd also been posting fliers at the grocery store and the laundromat advertising "potty-trained" kittens.

"He's just worried they won't get along with Goldie," she'd confided. "If we find them a family, he'll come around." She extolled the cats' beauty to anyone who would listen: people she met when she was hitting against the wall of the tennis courts at the park; the Sarconis' gardener, Frank Herrera; anyone else who happened to cross her path. Then one afternoon—I remember it was a Wednesday, the day I had to drag the garbage cans out to the street—my mother came into my room while I was cutting out photos of Mayan ruins for a social studies project. "Guess what?" she said, standing in the doorway in her bikini. "This Saturday we have a little surprise."

She had some kind of heavy cream all over her face, something she put on whenever she went out to the garden to take a sunbath. I asked her what kind of surprise.

"We have your friend Jason over for dinner," she said, giving me a sheepish grin.

"Jason? What do you mean?"

"Well, I know how much you like him, and I thought I surprise you by inviting his family over for dinner. I called his mother this morning."

"Are you insane?"

My mother insisted that she was just trying to be a good neighbor, but I knew what she was scheming. The thought of having her try to unload some of Sabine's cats on Jason's family, of having them watch my mother prance around in her dirndl, trying to yodel and telling the stories she always ended up telling complete strangers—stories about how, during the war, even a potato was a luxury and how the husbands of the women who hired her when she moved to America tried to have sex with her in the pantry or the gazebo or the garage—made me want to throttle her.

That night, I lay awake listening to the ticking of my clock. I heard my mother and Gerry go to bed, and in the distance I heard the sound of a train, like a foghorn out in the ocean. Periodically, I got up and turned on the light to see what time it was. I had a math test the next day, and I kept going over word problems in my head: questions involving the number of ice bricks necessary to build an igloo of a given size, or the quantity of paint required to cover a specified number of walls.

I thought about how my homeroom teacher, Mrs. Wilson, told me I was only allowed to ask her two questions per day and how she'd started making a clucking sound whenever I raised my hand. I remembered how even Jackie Fleischman, the girl with the leg brace, laughed when I asked Mr. Gutierrez whether something he'd said was going to be on the test. Recently I'd seen Jason hanging out with Sam Espinoza, a kid who carried his skateboard around with him all the time and who sometimes threatened to beat me up if I didn't give him a quarter. I wondered how long it would be until Jason figured out that everyone at school thought I was weird.

As it turned out, I didn't have to wait until Saturday for things to unravel. Two days later, I was walking home from school when I saw a police car in front of the Wallaces' house. Even from the top of the hill I could see the car's red and blue lights. School had ended an hour before, but I'd gone to the library to check out some books on Andrew Jackson. As I came down the hill, after it was too late to turn around and retrace my steps, I saw my mother and Sabine on the Wallaces' lawn, in their bikinis, being questioned by the police. Carol Wallace was standing next to them, gesticulating wildly while, to my horror, Jason and his sister stood on their porch, eating ice cream sandwiches and watching the spectacle unfold.

"Stewart!" my mother shouted. "Call Gerry. These men are trying to arrest us!" My mother's bikini was emergency orange, and the top was so tight the entire world could see her nipples. It was her favorite bikini, the one she called her *orange knockout*. Immediately I ran down the street, certain that Jason and his sister were watching me flee.

I arrived home out of breath and stormed through the house. Goldie got up from under the table and lumbered over to me, wagging her arthritic tail. "Out of the way, pig!" I yelled as I grabbed the phone and dialed Gerry's number. On the third ring, his secretary picked up and told me he was in a meeting. "Is there a message?" she asked.

"Can you tell him his wife called? She has a question about dinner."

When I hung up, I stood in the living room wondering what to do. Goldie was standing by the back door, staring at me. I looked at the bowl of lemons that my mother kept on the kitchen counter and the bottle of coconut suntan lotion. I imagined turning Goldie into a dragon and getting on her back and flying away. I wished I could turn the lemons into hand grenades and the suntan lotion into a flamethrower and burn Gerry's house to a crisp.

Sometimes I wished my mother had never met Gerry. I thought about how, when we first moved to L.A., my mother kept saying that the master bedroom, with its brown shag carpet and embroidered pillows, smelled like Gerry's wife, Fern, was hidden away in one of the closets, recently deceased. I remembered how my mother took all the sheets and blankets out of the bedrooms and washed them on hot, how she used so much detergent that it smelled like someone had dumped a bottle of perfume into the Maytag, how she kept the windows open all day, even when it was raining. I remembered her asking Gerry whether he appreciated everything she was doing to make his house nicer. *More livable* was the term she used. I remembered her getting up on the step stool with a bucket of bleach and scrubbing all the cupboards.

At first Gerry thanked her and said the house had needed a good cleaning, that he'd forgotten how dirty things can get if you don't stay on top of them. Then one day Gerry was in the family room, looking at his bookshelves, and he asked my mother where she'd put all his magazines. "Were you still reading those?" she asked. "I thought you were done with them, they were so full of dust. I put them in a shopping bag by the bikes. There was spider behind them I had to kill."

Gerry took off his Dodgers cap and rubbed his forehead. He stared down at the carpet and made the whistling sound he made whenever he was trying to act like everything was okay. "Is that where the photos are too? In the garage?"

"What photos?"

"Don't play dumb, Heike." I knew which photos he meant: the photos of Fern sitting in front of the fireplace wearing a New Year's hat, and Fern throwing a stick for Goldie at the beach, and Fern and Gerry with their sons, David and Rick, in front of Tomorrowland. The photo of everyone at Disneyland was my favorite. When we first moved to Gerry's house, I looked at that photo a lot. I wondered whether Gerry and Fern were good parents and whether David and Rick were happy growing up. I remembered trying to figure out what David and Rick were like back then, before their mother died. I wondered whether they were into fantasy games, or volleyball and skateboarding. The few times I'd met them, they both seemed quiet. Not nerdy quiet, just distracted, like they wanted to be somewhere else. In the photo they both seemed well-adjusted though. They were smiling and holding hands with Mickey Mouse. Gerry was giving Rick a piggyback ride, and Fern had her arm around David. For some reason I always ended up wondering whether Fern already had cancer growing inside her when that photo was taken. I often wondered whether my mother might have cancer or something else wrong with her; I wondered who would take care of me if she died.

"Did it ever occur to you that those photos might be important to me?" Gerry continued. He spoke slowly, enunciating each word carefully, as if his tongue caused him great pain. Then he went out to the garage, got the shopping bags, and brought them inside. I stayed on the couch in the family room, but I wasn't paying attention to the TV. I was waiting to see what Gerry would do. I was waiting to see whether Gerry would throw something at my mother and tell her to *fuck off*. That's what my real father would have done. He would have told my mother not to touch his fucking things ever again. Instead, Gerry got a dishtowel from the kitchen and wiped the photos. He held each frame carefully and ran the towel over the surface of the glass.

"I'm sorry," my mother finally said, starting to cry. "I shouldn't have put them away. I just couldn't stand it anymore, seeing Fern there every day, judging all the time from the grave."

Standing in the living room, I could tell Goldie wanted me to pet her. She was looking up at me, wagging her partially bald tail. I decided that, instead of going back to check on my mother, I would scoop up Goldie's droppings. It was the chore I hated most, the chore Gerry always had to remind me to do before I got my allowance. I opened the door to the yard, and Goldie followed me outside; even though she was old, she still liked to make her way over to the lemon trees and give them a sniff.

I walked to the grass with my plastic bag and the shovel, and I remember wanting to cry. The grass was brown, and some of the turds were so old that they looked like little pieces of wood. I retrieved the droppings with the utmost care, making the task last as long as possible. At one point, Goldie stood next to me, panting. Ten minutes later my mother and Sabine returned home.

"There you are," my mother yelled. "How dare you leave us stranded there on our own. Did you see the police? We could have been imprisoned!"

I told her I'd tried to call Gerry but that he was busy, and I was waiting for him to call back. I showed her what a good job I'd done cleaning the lawn. Sabine, whose hair was still damp, kept saying she wanted to be driven back to the motel.

That evening, Gerry laid into my mother. "I've had it, Heike! I can't live like this anymore!"

"How was I to know Carol would get home so early? We just went for a quick dip."

"By the way," I announced in the middle of their fight, "I'm not going to be here tomorrow for dinner."

"What do you mean?" asked my mother.

"I'm just not. I'm not going to sit here in front of Jason and his sister and act like everything is normal. They probably think you're a total retard."

"How dare you!" She lunged toward me, but I was too fast. I ran into my room and locked the door.

"Open this door and apologize to me!" she screamed. "I am your mother!" The more she pounded, the louder I turned up the radio. I sat at my desk trying to concentrate until, eventually, I put on my shoes. I emptied everything out of my backpack, took my life savings—$56.23—from the box I kept under my bed, and folded up three of my favorite T-shirts. I put the shirts in my backpack, along with the Dungeons & Dragons characters I'd painted by hand and a piece of turquoise my father had given to me as a present, and climbed out the window.

I moved fast, past house after house, afraid someone would catch me. When I reached the intersection at the top of the hill, I headed to Vons. I thought that, at a minimum, I'd need cereal for my trip. I walked to the aisle with the Fruit Loops and Lucky Charms and the other cereals my mother always said were too expensive, and as I studied the choices, I wondered whether I should have told Gerry and my mother where I was going. I imagined them pounding on my door, then picking the lock. I pictured my mother going berserk. I considered sneaking back to leave a note so she wouldn't worry. *I'll be okay. I'm going to Mrs. Moy's. Love, Stewart.*

Mrs. Moy was the woman who'd taught me Sunday school in Ventana Beach. She'd always told me that if I ever needed anything or if I was ever in trouble, I could give her a call. I didn't know her address, but I knew her number by heart. I went up to the cashier, gave her a box of Frosted Flakes, and handed her a ten-dollar bill.

"Do you mind giving me my change in quarters?" I asked.

"You bet, sweetie. You going to Vegas?"

I smiled, not sure what she meant, then headed to one of the pay phones, where I picked up the receiver and dialed Mrs. Moy's number. An automated voice told me I needed to put in ninety-five cents for the first three minutes, and after I deposited the coins, I listened to the phone ring. I let the phone ring at least twenty times before I finally hung up.

I watched the people in the parking lot put bags of groceries into the trunks of their cars. I wondered whether my mom and Gerry were watching the ABC Friday Night Movie, something about a woman who claimed her family was abducted by aliens. Eventually, I decided to walk to the beach. I'd walked to the ocean lots of times with my mother, and I remembered how each time we passed a particularly nice house, one of us would say that was the kind of home we wished we could live in. Some of the houses had elaborate gardens and pools and huge windows that allowed you to see into the living rooms and kitchens and dens. I thought about the children on the milk cartons. Every morning, when I was eating my Cheerios, I always stared at the black-and-white photo of whatever child was featured in that week's advertisement. The caption was always the same—Missing Child—but the details were different:

> Melinda Ramirez, Age 9. Last seen in El Cerrito Mall (June 23, 1975)
>
> Peter Yates, Age 7. Last Seen at Pismo Beach (March 13, 1973)

When I arrived at the bike path along the edge of the beach, I headed toward the pier. Occasionally I saw someone go by on roller skates or a bike, but for the most part the beach was deserted. The air on the pier felt cooler than I expected, and below me I heard the sound of the water. I sat at the end of the pier, letting my legs dangle over the edge and studying the oil derricks in the distance. I kept looking at my watch, wondering whether my mother and Gerry had figured out I was gone. I wished I'd brought a jacket along, instead of just my sweatshirt, and I tried to keep my legs as still as possible so I wouldn't get any splinters.

Eventually, a homeless guy with a sleeping bag and a fishing pole sat down on the pier and smiled at me. "How's it going, buddy?" he said. His teeth were brown and crooked, and he wore a shaggy beard. There'd been stories in the news about a man who strangled women in the Hollywood Hills and about a retired dentist in Arcadia who kept a twelve-year-old girl locked up in his cellar for ninety-six days, until she finally escaped when he went to the movies. I imagined the principal of my school telling everyone at Friday's assembly that my dismembered body had been found in a dumpster.

"What brings you out to these parts?" the drifter asked.

I pictured a hiding place under the pier where he forced people to have sex with him before he suffocated them. I wondered whether anyone would hear me if I screamed.

"Want a swig?" He offered me a bottle inside a paper bag.

I shook my head, looking down. My body felt light; suddenly I had to go to the bathroom. Without thinking, I leapt up, grabbed my backpack, and sprinted down the pier, toward the houses along the shore. I ran until I was sweating hard and my lungs felt raw and I reached a group of teenagers sitting on the strand smoking and laughing together. They looked at me and smiled, but I didn't stop. I climbed the huge hill leading from the train tracks to Sepulveda in record time. I pictured my mother on the couch, holding her wooden spoon, waiting. I decided to tell her that I'd snuck out of the house in order to buy her a gift.

Finally, when Gerry's house came into view, I saw that all of the lights were off except the one in my room. I hurried down the block and peered into my window. Miraculously, my room was exactly as I'd left it: the door was still locked, the folders and books I'd taken out of my backpack on the carpet next to my bed. I climbed back inside, my heart like a drum. A few minutes later, I turned out the light and got into bed. I held my breath, listening, but the house was perfectly quiet.

The next morning, when my alarm clock went off, I got dressed and went out to the living room like nothing had happened. "Thank you for saying goodnight," my mother called from the kitchen. "That was very nice of you."

I apologized, saying I'd fallen asleep while I was studying. "We don't have any more apples," she said, as she was making my lunch. "Is a banana okay? They're a little brown."

That afternoon, after I got home from school, I was in my room when Jason's mom, Mrs. McFarland, called to say they'd come down with the flu. "Are you happy?" my mother hollered. "Your friend cancelled! They're not coming over."

During the following weeks, I went out of my way to avoid Jason. I changed my route to and from school, and I spent as little time as possible in the hallways between classes. I took solace in the fact that next year Jason would be going to Tres Caminos High. As for Sabine, my mother's plan to have her move in never came to fruition. Two weeks after my mother and Sabine were almost arrested, as I was coming home from school, I saw my mother sweeping leaves in the driveway. She was wearing sunglasses, but I could tell she'd been crying. When I asked her how she was, she refused to look at me. "Fine," she replied.

"What's wrong?" I asked.

"Doesn't matter."

"What do you mean? What happened?"

"Nothing. Nothing happened." She kept sweeping the leaves, and I stood there looking at her. Finally she said, "Sabine is moving to Ohio. She decided to move back East to be closer to her cousin."

"Gosh. When did you find that out?"

"Little while ago."

"Really?"

"*Yes, really*. Stop pretending like you care about me. I know you don't give a damn." My mother started sobbing. "I just can't take it anymore." She let the broom fall onto the driveway. "One of these days, I move back to Germany."

I tried to calm her down. I asked her to tell me what Sabine had said, and then she told me the story. She said that Sabine never agreed to let her give any of the cats away and that, when my mother told her what she had in mind, she flipped out. "She accused me of trying to steal these pets from her. I told her this was not the case at all, but she wouldn't listen. I drove over there and tried to talk to her, but she was like a different person—so cold and icy. Her eyes were like rocks. Afterwards, I couldn't even drive I was so upset. I had to pull over into a gas station."

I stood under the huge willow tree outside Gerry's house, looking at my mother, wondering whether I should give her a hug. I knew she wanted me to cry with her, to tell her I loved her and no matter what, I would always be there for her. I knew she wanted me to reassure her that it didn't matter what Sandi Sarconi or Carol Wallace or Jason's mother thought of her. But I couldn't bring myself to say any of these things.

That December, amidst continuing news stories about Stockholm syndrome and the Symbionese Liberation Army, *Hotel California* hit the charts and *Rocky* and *King Kong* were released. The few times that I saw Jason over Christmas break, he was walking on the street with a girl who wore lots of lip gloss. By that point, I already knew that he'd climbed over the fence to retrieve his magazines. I'd gone out back one afternoon when my mother wasn't home, and all I found amidst the thicket of lemon trees were a few torn pages with part of an article about trout fishing and some photos of a woman sitting on the hood of a green Porsche. The paper was wet and discolored, and when I shook the leaves and dirt from the pages, a pill bug fell to the ground.

I brushed the dirt off the paper as carefully as possible and folded the pages. I surveyed the area to make sure I hadn't accidentally missed any remnants of the other magazines, then crept out of the tangle of branches and went back to my room. I closed my door, spreading the pages out on top of my desk and examining them, as if I were looking for some kind of clue. I knew that soon enough my mother would come home and start making dinner and that she would expect me to peel potatoes or make fruit salad or stir something on the stove so she would have someone to talk to.

1969

House
Made of
Snow

All evening, Stewart has behaved properly. Of this he is certain. Now it is late though, and night coaxes him into its arms. They are in his father's car, his mother in the front seat, he in the back, driving to his father's house in the country, where they will stay until morning.

Soon it will be Christmas, and this is a special occasion. His father invited them to a ballet, a performance with soldiers and swords and sugar plum fairies in flowing white gowns. "Promise me you do your best to be good," his mother instructed today, as they were getting ready to drive to his father's house from their apartment in Denver. His father lives at the edge of a forest with towering trees. "If he gives us the check, I buy you the coloring pens you want from the store." Heike had explained her plan to Stewart painstakingly, going over every detail. She needs his father to give them two thousand dollars so they can buy a new car and drive to California together. Otto, her bug, is too old to travel this great a distance.

The moon is full, the freeway empty and open. Looking out the window, Stewart conjures images of wild animals—a lion roaring into his face, a puma, black and sleek, chasing him in the night—but the car is warm, and his eyelids are heavy. Each time he drifts off, he catches himself. He knows his father doesn't want to have to carry him into the house.

The fields, covered in snow, glow under the sky. This is the time, Stewart knows, when fairies emerge from the woods and dance like confetti, when mice form their armies.

"I love *The Nutcracker* so much," his mother says. "They play it so beautiful." Stewart rests his cheek on the window's cold glass, feels the moon's palm on his skin.

"*Beautifully*," says his father, his voice like a blade.

"Beautifully," she repeats. Stewart says the word too, silently.

Sometimes, when he and his mother are driving at night, Stewart will point out things he sees in the distance. A caravan of elephants. A haunted castle. A giant octopus moving toward a river. Usually she'll play along, pretending to see the things he describes. Now, though, there is nothing outside. He does his best to keep watch, to find shapes in the fields—once or twice he spots a wolf or a fox or maybe a tiger crouching in the snow, then dashing for cover—but it becomes harder and harder to keep his eyes open.

"Stewart," his father says. "Wake up now, kiddo. Don't make me say it again."

His mother is sitting at the kitchen table, practicing the corrections his father wrote in pen on a sheet of lined paper.

The dog's fur is brown. (Never "The fur of my dog . . .")
There are three of us. (Never "We were three")
We were on the scooter, but then we got in the van. (In vs. On)
If I have enough butter, I will make a pound cake. (Not
    "would have")

I bought a new dress. How does it look? (Never "look like")
I feel happy today. (Never reflexive!)

She holds the paper in one hand and balances Stewart on her lap with the other. He watches her mouth as it moves, her cheeks and her chin, and he's reaching out to touch one of the curlers in her hair when a rat bursts through the window above the sink, its claws shattering the glass like a dragon enraged. The rat is large as a bear, yet what Stewart hears is not the sound of glass breaking, but something grating: the sound of wheels on gravel. Even before he opens his eyes, he knows they are close. He wills himself awake, sits up straight and tall.

The rat's bulging eyes, its pointed whiskers and teeth, the sharp claws, still inhabit his mind as he sees, through the window, the outline of soaring pine trees, so close he is certain their snow-covered branches will graze the car's body.

"There is nothing to be afraid of," his mother once told him. "The forest is full of magic and wonder. When I was a girl, Omi and I hiked for hours in the woods, collecting blueberries and strawberries and then, at the end of the summer, raspberries so ripe they turned to juice in your fingers. When we returned home, Omi put the fruit in a pot on the stove and boiled the berries with sugar until our tiny hut smelled like it was made from warm syrup."

Night air fills his lungs, like menthol or flames, and he waits next to his mother while his father opens the door. The house is a fortress of wooden beams and concrete, surrounded by bushes and shrubs covered in snow. Once they're inside, Stewart's mother folds his clothes, helps him put on the pajamas she brought over in her grocery store bag. His bed is a mattress laid out under a huge printing press, made—his father told him—in England during the reign of a king who beheaded nine men, including his own uncle and brother.

"Did he do his reading today?" his father asks.

His mother hesitates. "Today? Not today, but every other day we have been reading."

"Well, it has to be every day." His father stands like a warrior in his undershirt and white briefs.

Stewart knows what his mother is thinking. *First thing in the morning I must read with my son. There will always be groceries to buy and pants to wash out. Already his* walkjanker *is getting too small. I should have bought him something warmer in wool.*

"Stewart," his father says, "come here." He strides to the bookshelf and picks out *Grimm's Fairy Tales*. "Why don't we read one of these stories."

"But, Raymond, look what time it is. The boy should be already in bed."

"He's fine, Heike. Aren't you, kiddo? Come over here, son."

Stewart walks toward his father, whose undershirt is tight across the muscles of his chest. They sit on the couch, and his father asks which story he wants to read. Stewart studies the table of contents; the words seem to dance on the page.

"How about *Hansel and Gretel*?" his father asks. His mother has told him the story many times, each version slightly different from the previous.

His father finds the page and puts the book on Stewart's lap. Stewart's hands are already sweating. "Once upon a time," he begins, "there was a poor woodcutter who lived on the edge of a big forest"—he sounds each word out slowly, even the words he has seen before—"with his wife, who was not . . ." He pauses, looking at the word.

"You know this," says his father.

"Es-pe-k-a-ly," Stewart tries.

"*Especially*," his mother says. She is standing a few feet away, gripping her nightgown.

"Don't help him, Heike."

The next word is just as hard. Stewart isn't sure how to say it. He mouths the letters to himself, but everything jumbles. He knows what goes on in the story. It's about a mother and father who are poor and can't feed their children.

"Stewart, you've got to pay attention. This is only the first sentence."

"B-eee-out-i-ful," he says, sounding out the word almost inaudibly as the letters begin to float into the air.

"I can't hear you," his father says.

Stewart tries again, using all of his strength. He struggles to hold the pages in place, wills each letter still.

"B-EEE-OWT-I-FUL is not a word, Stewart. Do you know what B-EEE-OWT-I-FUL means?"

His body is hot, as if someone had turned on a furnace. His father's arm weighs down across his shoulders and neck.

"Raymond," his mother says. "Please. This is too much." Stewart knows his mother wants to say more. If she had gotten the money this afternoon, she could take Stewart and leave. *Why did I not ask for the check when my lipstick was nice and my hair had not flown away? Today was so windy. It made me a mess.*

"Quiet, Heike."

Stewart's throat contracts. If he lets even the smallest bit of air into his mouth, he knows he will cry. He strains to keep his eyelids wide, like a surfacing fish.

"Come on, Stewart. Start the sentence from the beginning, and think about what word makes sense in context."

Stewart reads the words to his father, one by one, making sure no letter moves. When he gets to *especially*, he freezes. He knows his mother just told him the answer. He makes the *e* sound and the *sp* sound. Then it happens again—the tail of the *y* curls up from the paper, reaching out toward him, like the tail of a lizard or an iguana or a black dragon. It lassoes his neck, tugging the *l* and the *a* and the *i*, pulling free from the page. He watches the letters peel up—the word, then the sentence itself, like a streaming ribbon, slippery as a minnow.

"Stewart! Don't fart around. You just said it."

Something breaks in his throat. His breaths come short and fast, like choking or the collapsing of lungs.

"Okay. That's it! Go outside until you calm down."

"Outside?" says his mother. "He can't go outside. It's the middle of the night!"

He's afraid his father might hit her. When his father starts yelling, his stubbled face often turns lava red.

"Outside, Stewart."

He feels the sounds coming out of his father's mouth. He gets up from the couch, his pajamas wet on his skin. His mother looks around for her shoes. He walks toward the front door, and she hurries over to him. She puts his arms into the sleeves of his jacket, then helps him open the door. She steps outside with him, but his father says, "No, Heike—you stay here." She pauses, looking at the man, then back at her son.

"You be okay," she says. "Nothing will happen. Think of what Mommy has said."

The air envelops him like a sea made of ice. His eyes adjust to the night. Above him, the sky glows with stars and the luminous moon: large and white and perfectly round.

Once there was a boy who was lost in the woods, and he walked and walked in the night. The villagers all thought he would not find his way home, and they took lanterns and went out into the forest to look for his footprints. Hour after hour, they searched for their Bübchen. *The later it got, the brighter became the stars and the moon. They cast light so the boy could see in the night, and they kept him company out in the snow. The boy did not grow afraid—he sang songs to himself, and, as he sang, the animals came out of the forest. The owls and squirrels and deer brought him baskets of food. Do not be afraid, the moon said to the boy. I am here to protect you.*

Stewart watches the moon. His mother is right. If you look closely enough, you can see a man's face. It smiles at him. He sees the stars stretching out toward him, reaching down through the trees. Inside the house he hears his mother crying. "Why are you like this to us? I made myself beautiful. Is this not the outfit you thought I should wear?"

He listens for his father's response but hears nothing at all. A few months ago, Stewart was visiting his father for the weekend, and they went to see *Mary Poppins*. His father bought him licorice and soda and told him they could sit in any seat Stewart chose. "I bet your mother doesn't buy you licorice when you go out," his father said. Later, as they were driving home, he asked Stewart a question: "Your mother still taking baths together with you? Tell me the truth."

Stewart didn't respond. His eyes were closed, and he was starting to dream. "I'm waiting, Stewart. Don't be like your mother now."

He wasn't sure what to say; he was thinking about the bubbles that piled up on top of the water. He liked it when his mother put a beard on his cheeks or a cap on top of his head. He was thinking about the way she poured the green gel into the water as it filled up the tub.

"It's okay, son. I know this hasn't been easy on you."

He wonders whether his father is standing on the other side of the door now, waiting. Perhaps he has gone into the bathroom to pick at his teeth. Maybe he will change his mind and make his mother stand outside too. If they both have to sleep in the woods, they can build a house made of snow, like the Eskimos do in the North. They can use branches from pine trees to keep themselves warm.

In the distance, the ground spreads out like a carpet of silver. The moon begins to approach, step by step. "Come closer," it beckons. "It's okay."

Stewart sees the branches in the woods sway back and forth. He wonders whether the trees move in the wind because they are trying to stand close together, for warmth, or whether they are trying to dance. *Each tree in a past life was a famous ballerina who was graceful and nimble and beautiful.*

Stewart is at the far end of the gravel driveway when he hears his father call his name. He stops, the voice distant and small. "Stewart?" his father repeats. "You still out here, kiddo?"

He turns and sees the man, in socks, in the doorway, a half figure looking into the darkness. "You better come back inside. It's getting late. I made up your bed."

"We're waiting for you," the moon says to him. "The dancers are ready to start." Up ahead, he sees two reindeer come out from the bushes, and several squirrels; they are carrying something for him, a basket of *Zwetschgenkuchen* and *Pfeffernüsse* and perhaps something else. He walks quickly, snow thick underfoot, his father's words lost in the night.

1988

The Lure

In a matter of weeks, it seemed, Stewart's mother had become obsessed with the dog. Despite—or maybe because of—the fact that he, Banjo, didn't belong to her. Things like that didn't matter to Heike: who was the rightful owner of something, of a pet or a piece of property. She had no sense of boundaries or decorum. She liked to be in charge, to exercise control. Over pets, renters, people she came across at Vons or Taco Bell, over Gerry, over her twenty-four-year-old son, an adult the last time he checked.

Heike lived in California; Stewart lived in New York, where he was in grad school, studying oppression and alienation and identity politics. He loved New York, loved sitting in his room overlooking Amsterdam Avenue, listening to the traffic—the sirens and horns—reading until midnight, then going out to the bars. He took the subway downtown. This was back when going to Avenue C felt dangerous, when you could go to Save the Robots at 3:00 in the morning and not leave until guys in suits were going to work. He went to Boy Bar and Crowbar and Boiler Room.

Recently he'd started going to the Lure. They had a dark room where people hooked up. You could meet someone by the pool table or the pinball machine, chat for a few minutes, then go to the back. You didn't even have to chat if you didn't want to. You could just stand in the dark and wait for someone to come up to you. You could suck a stranger's dick, no questions asked. There were plenty of guys: guys with tattoos and pierced nipples, guys with buckteeth, skinheads. He liked it all.

If it was up to him, he wouldn't have come home for Christmas. He would have stayed in New York. But it wasn't up to him. His mother had guilt-tripped him into visiting for ten days, six days more than seemed reasonable, or prudent. Gerry had been diagnosed with lymphoma seven months earlier and had just finished several rounds of chemotherapy. "Don't you love me?" Heike asked on the phone. "Don't you want to see us?"

So here he was, in the passenger seat of her hatchback, driving down the 101 from Gerry's ranch house toward his mother's condo, the place he and his mother had lived in together when he was eight, nine, ten years old, after his parents' divorce, after he and his mother moved to Ventana Beach to start a new life together, to find his mother a decent husband, to find *happiness*.

Heike's plan, today—because she always had something in mind, some kind of plan or angle—was to take back a certain set of dishes she'd bought at Pottery Barn, a very expensive and beautiful set of plates and cups and bowls she'd lent Linda Montgomery, his mother's current renter, out of the goodness of her heart. At least that's what she'd said. But Stewart wasn't a fool. He knew his mother wasn't going to the condo just for the dishes. Odds were that Banjo would figure in somehow.

This morning, before Stewart was awake, Heike had come into his room, the room she called his room, despite the fact that it was full of cuckoo clocks and dolls she'd bought in Munich and carried with her on the plane so they wouldn't be damaged. "Come on sleepie boopie!" she called out to him. "Time to get up. It's a nice day outside!" Her voice was like something out of a sitcom. She was the woman who wouldn't take no for an answer, who was dressed at 7 A.M., wondering why everyone was still in bed.

Apparently, the guy she usually played tennis with on Thursdays had cancelled, and she wanted Stewart to hit backhands to her on the public courts. She wanted him to spend time with her, because she never saw him, and he was her son. Stewart pulled himself together and got dressed and played tennis with his mother. They practiced backhands, then they went to Sears to return a comforter that Heike bought maybe a decade ago, and now here they were in her car, driving south, to the condo to ransack Linda's apartment—to unlock the front door and go into the poor woman's kitchen and pack up her dishes and then, in all likelihood, engage in other pernicious activities.

Walking Banjo was the thing that had caused the fight with Linda in the first place, Linda having caught Heike taking Banjo to the beach without permission. Heike had told Stewart the story more than once. He knew all about Linda's outburst and her ungrateful attitude and un-Christian demand that Heike refrain from going into her apartment when she was at work and taking her dog to play in the ocean. "Here I give her this beautiful garden and she keeps the poor thing cooped up in the kitchen," Heike had said. "It's ridiculous. The dog goes crazy in there all by himself."

Now Linda was threatening to move out, despite having signed a two-year lease, despite the fact that Heike had spread out the red carpet for her.

It wasn't the first time Heike had fought with one of her renters. Before Linda, a guy named Saul, a Christian Scientist from Oxnard, lived in the condo. He and Heike had been arguing about how much hot water he was using. Then one day he came home for lunch and found her lying in the yard, naked, on the chaise longue. She didn't think it was a big deal, going over there without his permission and taking off all her clothes.

If Stewart were to ask his mother why she insisted on going over to someone else's apartment when that person, the rightful occupant, was not home, she would, invariably, give him an earful. "It's my home," she'd say. "I miss it. Why should he care if I go for a sunbath when he's gone? We made a deal. I gave him $50 off on the rent." Then she'd pause and, if she didn't like her interlocutor's demeanor, she'd ask, "Whose side are you on anyway?"

"We're in luck," Heike said as they pulled into the carport. "She's not here."

Heike had promised Stewart they'd be home by 12:30, at the latest, and here it was already 12:56. Stewart wanted to go home and take a shower and start his day. He was hungry, and he had things to do. He needed to write a paper about transgression and repression in Foucault, a fitting topic if you thought about it. He needed to impress his advisor so he could keep his fellowship so he'd keep getting the $863 check his department had been putting in his mailbox on the first of each month.

"Why do you always have such a long face?" his mother asked after she turned off the engine. "Aren't you happy to be here?"

"I'm elated."

"Don't be such a snob. Come on and meet this little pumpkin."

"I really don't think you should keep going into her place."

"My God. Okay. I go on my own." She opened the car door and gave him a look. "You know, I've been through a lot the last six months. The least you could do is be a little helpful the few days you're here."

Stewart waited in the car, seat belt still on, contemplating his mother's intractable nature, and Gerry's cancer, and the drag show he'd seen at Boy Bar last week. On the one hand, she was right, she had been through a lot: taking Gerry to the hospital every other week, waking up in the middle of the night to clean up his vomit. On the other hand, she specialized in being a pain in the ass. The night before, she'd insisted on having Stewart sit on the couch with her to watch *Gone with the Wind*. Then, when he kissed her goodnight, she started crying. "What did I do to make you hate me so much?" she asked.

"I don't hate you," he said. She was wearing a nightgown— something not quite sheer, but thin, too thin for the situation at hand—and he felt her breasts pressing against him. He stood there, staring at the fake Christmas tree, the tree his mother stored in the shed with the spiders and mice, looking at the blinking lights and trying not to pull away too quickly. His mother drove him crazy, but he knew that, for the most part, she couldn't help it.

Before she met Gerry, Heike had dated a string of losers—insurance salesmen whose ex-wives had restraining orders against them, mechanics who were broke and who knocked on the door late at night when they were horny. She and Stewart moved from apartment to apartment, until she finally scraped together enough money to make the down payment on the condo. His dad's child support and alimony checks were always late, but Heike wanted Stewart to have his own room, so she let him sleep in the bed and she slept on a piece of foam next to the dresser. In the morning, she rolled up the mat and put it in the closet. Gerry was the best of the lot: he worked at a mortgage company, paid his bills on time, didn't get mad when Heike was having her period.

After *Gone with the Wind*, after Heike's tears and the hugging, it took Stewart forever to fall asleep. He kept thinking about a guy he'd met at the Lure, a guy from Yugoslavia who'd invited him back to his place on the Lower East Side and tried to get him to drink his warm piss—directly. He lived in a fifth-floor walk-up with a fire escape overlooking a playground. He had a Prince Albert and wrists as thick as Stewart's biceps.

He made it clear who was the boss, who was going to do the fucking. "Shut up," he said at one point when Stewart tried to resist. Stewart must have known what was going to happen, must have sensed that this guy wasn't going to send him home with a box of homemade cookies. He was hotter than any guy Stewart had ever hooked up with, and Stewart kept wondering whether he'd see him again.

Sure enough, when Heike emerged from the condo, she had the dog in her arms. The dog wasn't huge, but he was too big to carry, and here he was squirming and yelping and struggling to get free. "Will you please get out of the car?" Heike yelled.

Stewart looked at her through the windshield, with its dead flies and bird crap, then unfastened the seat belt.

"Look how cute this furball is," she said.

Stewart went over and admired the dog. "Feel his fur," she insisted. "Touch him." Heike had been talking about getting a new dog for a while. The dog she adopted when Stewart moved to college—an Australian shepherd with different-colored eyes—now had difficulty moving his bowels.

Banjo was a mutt. He had burrs in his fur. "Do you want to hold him?" she prodded. "Come on—I have to go big."

Stewart told himself not to get worked up. He told himself he should be loving and caring and grateful for everything his mother had done for him since he was a little boy. He held the dog, then put him down to see if he'd learned how to sit. He looked at the dog's leather collar. "You have a nice neck," the guy from Yugoslavia had said. Stewart liked his hands, the way his nails were bitten. The guy had muscles on his stomach and calluses on his palms.

"Banjo!" Heike called out a few minutes later, carrying a shopping bag with the plates and bowls and God knows what else. "Walk time!" Immediately, the dog began to yelp as if someone had put a match to his tail.

His mother went to the backseat of the car and took out a soiled red leash. The dog was jumping up and down, barking like a maniac. Stewart reminded her what Linda had said.

"Have you no heart?" Heike shot back. "Don't you see how he suffers?"

They walked down the street—Stewart and his mother and Banjo—past dumpsters full of cardboard boxes and bags of trash, past a VW bug with a cracked windshield, past the white mobile home that had been parked in the cul-de-sac for as long as he could remember. Banjo strained to sniff things: flowering ice plant, an empty can of Goya beans, a rusted propeller.

"Look how strong he is," Heike said, bracing herself to stop him from climbing onto the ivy. She was full of admiration.

She reached down to pet him, lowering her face to his, letting him give her a lick. The dog lay on his back, spread-eagle, while she cooed to him, petting his belly. "My goodness. *Du bist ein süsses Kind.*"

The skin on her hands and arms looked more wrinkled than he remembered. "You need a little loving, right *mein Schatz?*" she said. The dog was writhing on the pavement, going crazy, his penis shiny and red.

It occurred to Stewart then that the reason he had not come out to his mother probably had very little to do with his fear of rejection but rather with the fear that coming out to her would allow her to insinuate herself more fully into his life. She was the kind of person who would tell you whether her period was late, whether the man she'd just gone on a date with was skilled at making love and, if so, in what ways. Stewart was not interested in having Heike ask him questions about his personal life, about the things people wanted him to do on the roofs of their buildings. He didn't want her sending him articles about Rock Hudson and Patient Zero.

They took the shortcut to Josten's, an electronics company built on a hill overlooking the ocean. They cut through some bushes, crossed two more streets, then headed up the winding road, lined with large eucalyptus trees, that led to the parking lot, an expanse of asphalt surrounded by manicured lawns and glass buildings full of people minding their own business. People in button-down shirts who knew what was expected of them.

"Look at the ocean," Heike said when they reached the place with the best view. "Isn't it beautiful?" It was 1:47 P.M. Stewart was starving.

Here they were, his mother in her white tennis skirt, he in his yellow shorts and tennis shoes that were two sizes too large. His legs were skinny and pale, and the skin on his right knee was ashen, and he was wearing a thick pair of hiking socks so that his feet didn't bounce around in his dying stepfather's Tretorns. Stewart told his mother he was hungry; he reminded her that she'd broken her promise to let him work on the outline for the paper he needed to write; he said enough was enough.

"What if Linda comes home and finds out?" he pleaded.

"Ach, it's not even two. She stays at work until five. Don't always worry so much. Enjoy the scenery—smell the fresh air. You never know how long we all have." The sky was clear, and in the distance the ocean seemed to stretch out forever. Something about the ocean was peaceful and reassuring. If nothing else, it was a place he could drown himself.

"Be happy you don't have cancer," his mother said. "Dr. Karlow told me there's a fifty-fifty chance Gerry won't make it."

"But he was talking about going skiing."

"You're catching him at a good time. You should have been here six weeks ago. He looked like a corpse." Just this morning

Gerry had been up for breakfast and had gone outside, in his lime-green hat—the hat Heike had bought for him for a buck fifty at Goodwill—and worked on trimming the hedges. Stewart watched him, through the sliding door that led to the yard. Stewart saw him moving slowly, as if he were trying to walk along the bottom of a swimming pool. Gerry seemed to be examining the leaves, looking for some kind of fungus or abnormal growth.

Now, here, Banjo was tugging at the leash, a stick in his mouth. "Let's let him off, so he can run a bit," Heike said, bending down to unfasten the clasp. Stewart tried to say something, to point out the various No Trespassing signs. He told her they'd already pushed their luck, reminded her that people could see them.

"Come on," she said. "Just for a minute. He needs exercise."

Stewart wondered whether he'd let the Yugoslavian go too far, whether he needed to get tested. The guy had told Stewart to get down on all fours. "Like this," he said, rearranging Stewart's limbs. His apartment smelled like turpentine, and the wood on the floors was splintering. All he had in his fridge was a jar of pickles and three slices of bread.

The second the dog was free, he made a beeline for a group of seagulls that had settled near one of the picnic tables. The birds exploded into the air, sending Banjo into a spasm of howls. Stewart ran toward him, calling his name. The dog couldn't care less. He trotted over to the bicycle rack, threw a glance in Stewart's direction, then proceeded to take a dump.

"*Look,*" Stewart called out to Heike, who was now sitting on one of the benches, putting on lipstick. "Look what he's doing!"

His mother played dumb, smiling—at him, at Banjo, at the seagulls. Then she closed her purse and stood up. "My goodness. He must have had to go badly."

"Well, we can't just leave it there."

"You always go by the book," she said, heading over to a garbage can, where she retrieved a paper cup and some newspaper. She walked over to Banjo's feces. Stewart was a good twenty feet away, but the smell of the dog's shit still filled his lungs. As his mother struggled to maneuver the droppings with the edge of the cup, her tennis skirt hiked up so that Stewart could see her underwear. He looked away at the grass, tried to see something else, anything, but it was too late; he couldn't get the flash of his mother's crotch out of his head, her panties and stray pubic hair.

They spent the next twenty minutes yelling Banjo's name. The dog liked to run—he wasn't picky about destination: the flower-beds along the main building, the area with the petunias and the begonias and the other plants that were meant to be undisturbed, the picnic tables, the trash bins and bicycle rack. Eventually, he ran down the hill, into the wooded area closer to town. Stewart followed his mother, full of despair, listening to her calls. Part of him wanted something terrible to happen to Banjo and to her, to everyone involved. He wanted the guilty to be punished.

"Shit!" Heike shouted halfway down the hill. She was trying to traverse an off-kilter fence. "I hurt myself! Can you please come down here and help me?"

"Coming!" Stewart yelled back, hurrying to help her navigate the barbed wire.

"If this dog gets hit by a car, I never forgive myself."

"Don't worry so much. *He needs exercise.*"

"Don't be so fresh. Now go down there to the road to make sure he's not there. I'll go around the other side."

"He probably already went back to Linda's. We should see if he's there."

"That's ridiculous. He's a young dog. He's out having fun."

"So you want me to go where?"

"To the road," she said, pointing. "There's traffic down there."

Stewart walked down the hill to the side of the road, holding the leash, the image of his mother's panties still lodged in his brain. Here he was, again, on full display, for everyone to see. He looked like a complete dork.

Up the street, a blond guy was barreling down the hill on a skateboard. He was wearing flip-flops and looked like he'd just finished doing a Calvin Klein underwear shoot. Stewart fixed his eyes on the asphalt, hoping to make himself smaller and less conspicuous. He heard the sound of the skateboard's wheels on the macadam and the whoosh as the surfer whizzed past. Because clearly this guy surfed. Clearly this guy went to the beach every day, with his wetsuit and his surfboard and his girlfriend.

Stewart stared at his legs—tan, muscular, flexed—then al-lowed himself to imagine the surfer above him, straddling him, giving him orders. Stewart watched him disappear around the bend. He wondered whether maybe, on his way to the beach, he was going to stop at the Baskin-Robbins down the road. Stewart knew the place was still there. He'd liked going there when he was a child. He and his mother would go to the beach together, and, sometimes, if he pleaded enough, she'd buy him a scoop on the way home. She'd let him choose the flavor, but, invariably, she ended up asking for bites.

It was now 2:41. His stomach was churning with acid and bile, and there was really no point in standing on the road, in the sun, looking like a moron, so he walked down to the store and ordered a sundae with pecans on top. He'd warned his mother sufficiently. There was nothing left for him to do but see how things played out.

He still had the leash in his hand, and he was fingering the metal clasp. He was leaning against the glass case, watching the girl scoop Rocky Road. She was meticulous, which he liked, and for some reason what he thought about then was his father, his real father, and how he used to make his mother cry, about the way Heike looked when she was standing in the kitchen of the condo, calling Raymond on the phone, pleading with him to send money. Stewart remembered her sitting on the Formica countertop, twisting clumps of her hair—long and naturally red then— remembered having to get on a plane to visit his father, crying all the way down to LAX, his mother stroking his head, telling him everything was going to be okay. "The summer won't be that long. Soon you'll come home, and we'll be together again."

He remembered how, after school, she picked him up near the playground and they went to Kmart together, where they walked up and down the aisles and she tried on outfits she couldn't afford. He remembered her telling him stories about her life in Germany during the war—about having to sneak out to the field with a burlap sack to steal grass for the rabbits, about the man with the limp who patrolled the perimeter, looking for thieves—the way her reflection looked in the mirror of their bathroom while she was doing her hair. She'd stand in front of the sink, in her underwear, putting in her curlers, and he'd kneel on the pink toilet seat, looking at her, telling her what his life was going to be like when he was an adult. He was going to be rich and powerful, and they were going to live in a castle together, surrounded by a moat with a drawbridge.

Stewart was just starting to eat the sundae when he saw his mother stumbling down the street, pulling Banjo by the collar, glaring at him as he came out the front door. "What on earth are you doing?" she shouted. "Are you crazy? Don't you know we have a crisis on our hands!"

"Sorry. I was trying to find you. I didn't know where you were."

"Trying to find me! In the ice cream parlor?"

By then everyone was staring and he'd begun to smell something—something caustic, like ammonia or sulfur.

"This dog has gotten in trouble!" she yelled. "He got sprayed by a skunk! Now give me the leash before he gets away one more time."

His mother's hair had come out of its ponytail and was frizzier than ever. She looked wild.

"His entire body is covered!" she screamed. "We have to hose him off quickly!"

The dog's eyes were watering and swollen, and he kept rubbing his snout with his paws. Heike yanked the leash out of Stewart's hands and attached the clasp to Banjo's collar. "*Böser Hund.* Here I try to do something nice, and God spits down on me!"

The dog trailed her up the hill, ears hugging his skull, while Stewart hurried to keep up, eating his sundae as quickly as possible.

"Put that down and make sure this dog doesn't move," she said when they reached Linda's place. She handed him the leash, then disappeared inside the condo.

The stench coming from the dog was terrible. Stewart tried to hold his breath as long as he could. He wondered whether this was what mustard gas smelled like, whether this was what soldiers in the trenches had been forced to endure. He wondered what would become of his mother and of Gerry and of himself. They would all die, eventually, but what would happen before that, before their respective deaths?

How would he, for example, get from point A to point B? Would Gerry die first and leave his mother distraught? He'd played out the various permutations again and again in his head: Heike showing up on his doorstep in New York, unhinged, trying to move in with him. Heike forcing him to move home to Ventana Beach and comfort her, insisting that he sit with her on the couch that had begun to reek and watch TV together, sit with her at the dining room table, bathe her when she was too old to care for herself. Perhaps the situation would be reversed and she would end up caring for him. He thought of the covers of *Time* and *Newsweek*, the photos of emaciated men with sunken cheeks, like Holocaust victims, in hospital beds.

Eventually, his mother emerged from the condo with a bottle of shampoo and a pink towel. "Guide him over to the hose now! We don't have much time."

"This is why I hate coming home," Stewart yelled back.

"Do you think I wished for this outcome? I still have to cook my rouladen and make the red cabbage." Then she turned on the hose. The water made the dog jump, at which point she insisted that Stewart hold Banjo's collar. The dog locked his legs, trying to pull away.

"Come on, you," she shouted, kneeing him in the side. He yelped, then moved forward. "Wet him down now," she said, handing Stewart the hose as she squeezed green gel onto the dog's fur. Stewart wondered whether an angel might come down from the Heavens and grant them, each of them, forgiveness and succor.

It was a beautiful day, and, as Heike was working the shampoo into Banjo's coat, the sun lit up her hair. Stewart saw the gray roots and the patches of gray near her ear. He knew that she colored her hair at home, using a cheap product purchased at Sav-On, and he wondered whether, if one day he was responsible for her care, she would ask him to dye her hair for her. Something was wrong with the skin under her neck, near her ears—it looked splotchy and scarred, undoubtedly from the facelift she'd gotten. Sometimes scar tissue tingled in the night and caused pain. He wondered whether he would be asked to knead this skin with his hands should it become too painful for her to endure. Would there be a time when he would end up being, as she'd always claimed, all she had?

After she finished drying the dog, his mother stood up. She had mud on her legs, and the dog still reeked. "Blach," she said. "You are a very bad dog causing all these problems for me."

Banjo looked at her and tried to lie down in the mud.

"No!" she screamed, jerking him toward the pavement. "I've had it with you!" She gave him a smack on the rear, then used the towel to wipe the mud off his belly. "Go inside and get me some of this nice perfume she keeps in the bathroom. Make sure you take off your shoes."

"Sure. Great. Let's all trespass wherever we want."

"Fine, be this way," his mother said. She pulled the dog toward the yard. "Get in there!" she yelled, shoving him and closing the gate.

Then she spotted the dish of melted ice cream on the hood of her car. "Are you finished with this now?" she asked, picking up what was left of the sundae. She stood there, next to her car, spooning the chocolate into her mouth. In the background, Banjo whined and scratched at the fence.

Stewart wondered if the guy from the Lure had meant what he said. He told Stewart he'd been a good boy. He made Stewart coffee and toast. Afterwards, when Stewart was walking to the subway, he smelled the guy on his clothes—his sweat and his semen. He had a musky scent that Stewart wished were his own. For days, he wore the same shirt, refusing to wash it. He sat in the library, studying particles of dust float up and then down, dancing in the light that came in through the windows.

Stewart watched his mother devour the remains of his lunch. In one minute, it would be four o'clock. He had to go to the bathroom, but he kept his mouth shut. He wasn't going to use Linda's toilet. He told his mother that he was feeling sick, that he needed to get home right away, that if she didn't get in the car immediately, he'd go down to the corner and call a taxi. "I don't give a fuck about the towels," he was saying when he saw a pickup truck speeding toward them.

Before she'd even turned off the engine, Linda was screaming at the top of her lungs. "Heike! So help me God, if you've been walking Banjo again, you're going to regret it!"

"Hello, Linda," Heike said brightly, wiping a drop of chocolate from her top. "Merry Christmas!"

"Don't Merry Christmas me. Ellen Jiménez told me she saw you out with my dog!" Linda was a squat woman, pit bull—like, her cheeks covered with pockmarks. She stormed over to Banjo—

who was barking nonstop—gave him a quick look, then headed for Stewart and his mother. She was carrying a large bag of candy canes.

"I've done nothing at all," Heike said. "I simply come here to water the plants. You know very well how little rain we've had this past month."

"Don't fucking lie to me, Heike." Linda was just a few feet away now, and Stewart wondered whether she might slug his mother.

"How dare you use this kind of language with me," Heike said, taking a step back and opening the car door. "I am your landlady. I have no interest in this dog of yours."

"That's right. Banjo is my dog. *Mine.*"

"Then maybe you should take him out for a walk once in a while!"

"It's none of your business," Linda shouted, lunging forward and hurling the candy canes against the trunk of their car. Heike jumped back.

"You really have balls, you know that. I'm having the locks changed. I'm having the locks changed, and I'm calling the police. I'm going to get a restraining order against you. Next time you come over here without my permission, I'm going to have you arrested."

And that was it. Linda didn't slug his mother or yank her hair. She didn't pull out a gun or a chainsaw. She simply went into her apartment and slammed the door.

"Are you okay?" Stewart asked, once they were both in the car.

He wanted to say something else, felt he ought to say more. There was so much he could have said to her then, so much he could have told her. Not just about the Yugoslavian guy, but about the Puerto Rican guys who called him *papi* and the guy with dreadlocks from the Bronx who took him to Coney Island to ride the Cyclone. About the fact that sometimes, after he talked to his mother on the phone, he sat on his bed and cried. Because part of him did miss her, and because he often wondered whether she was right, whether he was a bad son.

"Okay? My husband's dying of cancer. My son despises me. Why should I be okay?"

Stewart wasn't sure what to say. He allowed himself to look at his mother then, not her face exactly but her mouth and the mole on her chin. She was wearing a necklace—a thin gold necklace that she'd had for decades. It wasn't valuable, but she'd always been careful with it. When he was a child, she'd asked him to help her with the clasp when she was putting it on, and she bent down so that his fingers could pull the tiny lever and attach the two interlocking pieces, right there, on the back of his mother's neck. If she'd sprayed Aqua Net in her hair, that smell would fill his lungs and leave him light-headed.

He knew what his mother wanted to hear, but, instead of comforting her, he sat in the car next to her, unable, unwilling to respond. He put on his seat belt and looked out the window. He stared at the condo's orange door and the ivy on the hill and, above the hill, the cloudless sky. By this point, Heike was crying. She told him that she knew all the neighbors there hated her and that Ellen Jiménez had always been jealous of her and that no matter what she did she never got a break. She asked Stewart whether he thought she'd done anything wrong, whether it was wrong of her to want to help Banjo.

Then she turned on the engine and backed the car up, and before they headed down the street, she put her hand on his leg. "You're all I have, Stewart. We're family. One day you'll understand what that means."

The car was hot, and he felt her skin on his skin, both of them still smelling of skunk and dog and Linda's shampoo. Those smells of ammonia and sulfur and apple, and of the cloying green air freshener that hung from her rearview mirror—something that didn't smell like pine trees or evergreen or anything natural—stayed with him, and he rolled down the window, craving fresh air.

Enormous
in the
Moonlight

Mein lieber Sohn,

It is Christmastime here again, the time of year I miss you the most. All day I spend baking Reindeer cookies and one Stollen after another. Already I have baked nine loaves and have four more to put in the oven. Each year, the list of recipients grows longer and longer.

Yesterday I ran into Lana Horton at the mall when I was buying Gerry new underpants. Do you remember her? I barely recognized the woman she is so gray nowadays. She uses a walker and goes very slowly. I almost didn't say hi, I was in such a rush, but she waved and called out my name.

For more than thirty minutes she talked my ear off, telling me about her arthritis and the lump on her breast she had removed, then showing me photos of her granddaughter who gave a recital last week of Mozart's Piano Sonata in C. This brought tears to my eyes, because I remembered her teaching you *Für Elise* so long ago, and the little Sonatinas you were so good at. Finally, she asked how you were, which of course was too much to bear. Apparently she had not heard the news, and I did not have the energy to explain everything. I said you were fine, still living in Boston as a professor, and she was very impressed.

What on earth could I tell the poor soul? My son, who had everything handed to him on a silverplatter, including a college degree, a good job, nice apartment, and loving mother, decided out of the blue to swallow a bottle of pills? She would never have understood why someone with so much privilege and good luck could possibly do this.

If anyone was to throw out the towel, it should have been me. Do you not remember how much I endured from childhood on? Yes, you had these bullies chasing you after school, but this is nothing compared to having bombs fall on one's head from the sky. Imagine being forced to flee your home at the tender age of five. I must have narrated for you how Omi woke Dieter and me at one in the morning and told us we had to dress immediately. She forced me to leave everything behind—my dolls and beautiful outfits, and even my little white kitten, Schneeflocke, whom I received as a gift for my birthday. I cried and cried as we went through the streets to the train station. All around, buildings were burning and people smashed windows to steal loaves of bread and vegetables and whatever else they could carry.

The station was crowded like Satan himself was arriving, everyone huddled together in the freezing cold hoping the train would arrive finally. We three squeezed close, seeking warmth from each other until, eventually, there came the big engine and everyone pushed towards the track because they were afraid there would not be enough room in the cars. We rushed for the doors but very few could get on, so people started climbing through the windows and, as they climbed in, those on the ground tried to steal their shoes. Just making it aboard in one piece was a miracle.

Of course there were no seats to be had, so we pressed against each other like sardines in a tin. I stood next to a fat woman and her husband who smelled like *Leberkäse* and who put little pieces of chocolate into his mouth, without offering one crumb to anyone. Going to the bathroom was impossible, of course, and we were forced to hold our bladders as long as we could, steering clear of the metal bucket they passed around. I kept trying to peer out the window, hoping to see the mountains Omi had told us about, until eventually she pointed out these monstrous things in the distance, enormous in the moonlight.

When Garmisch came, we were completely exhausted, but still we had to trudge nearly an hour through the snow to the cottage that was our new home. Omi could barely open the gate the banks were so high. I remember she went out to the pump for a cup of water to make us something to eat, and all we had was one bowl that was dented and half a dozen bitter turnips she brought along in a sack. Fortunately Omi had with her some matches and she found a few sticks of wood to make a small fire. She boiled water with these turnips and this was our meal. We were terribly hungry there so many nights. Each week Omi got just one loaf of bread with the coupon she received and she cut slits on the top to show how much we could eat every day. She covered the loaf with a dishtowel, and sometimes Dieter and I would look up at it with our mouths watering, hoping for one extra slice.

Luckily Omi made friends with a farmer down the road and knitted blankets for him in exchange for some rabbits that we kept outside in the garden. Once a month she killed one for us to gorge ourselves on. She took it out of the cage by its hind legs and we always watched it struggle for freedom. The rabbit's nails were actually quite long and sometimes they scratched Omi's arm and we became very alarmed seeing her bleed. Nothing bothered her though. She took the rabbit and banged its head against a big rock and cut into the fur with her kitchen knife. Then came the part we salivated for, putting this rabbit meat into a pot with some water and whatever vegetables she was able to get and, if we were lucky, some potatoes. We went crazy smelling such good food in our house. Without the rabbits we might have died.

Did I ever tell you one night two Jewish boys came into our garden to steal our biggest rabbit whom we called Wittekind? It was just after the war, when Hitler was finally dead, and there came these two boys one afternoon talking to us. Ahh, they said to me over the fence, and what have you there? They saw our cages with rabbits and made conversation about them. They couldn't have been more than sixteen or seventeen, but to me they were terrifying with their shaved heads and their skinny skinny bodies. In those days, we had no idea what horrible things had gone on, burning people in ovens and melting teeth down for gold.

That night Omi was sleeping with the door open and she heard Wittekind scratching inside his cage. What are you doing here? she screamed after these two boys and she schussed them away with a broom, but one of them had a knife and he turned against her. To this day I don't know how she survived. She screamed bloody murder and forgot her own fear because when you make a lot of noise you scare your own terror away. All she could think about was protecting our Sunday dinner.

Dieter must have been not more than twelve or thirteen, and I was just nine, and we watched from inside the house. The next day when she asked us to fill these two sacks she kept under the sink with grass for the rabbits we had no complaints. We were grateful to have her alive.

If it is true there is an afterlife, perhaps you have become friends with Omi by now. I know that when she came to visit us in Gerry's house, you always felt like she judged you for wanting these peach yogurts when you got home from school, but I hope you don't hold this against her. From her perspective, food was not to be taken for granted. In any case, you can't hold grudges forever. If you see her, please, for my sake, be kind. It is the least you can do for me now.

I wish so much you could write a letter to me and explain what life is like after death. Do you live in your own apartment in Heaven? Do you cook your own meals and go grocery shopping? I sometimes picture it like a big college, with dormrooms and a cafeteria, though if this is the case, I hope you are not as picky about the angels' cooking as you were with mine. Do they make this tofu you always insisted on having, and tasteless brown rice?

Sometimes at night I walk out to the mesa and look up at the sky full of stars and I wonder what you are doing. I picture you sitting in a big comfy armchair, reading one of your books. Perhaps by now you have started getting gray hair. I hope that when my time comes, the angels will allow me to live in the same neighborhood as they put you. Don't worry, I won't insist on sharing a bedroom together! I know you need your own space. It is fine with me that I live a few blocks away. This way at least I can stop by and just say hello every once in a while. It would be nice to see you again, even if for just a short time.

Love from your
Mutti

1994

Outside
Is the
Ocean

The man offers him a drink. Gin and tonic? Bourbon? Cognac? Stewart isn't much of a drinker. "Whatever you're having," he says, standing in the living room, awkwardly, looking over the harbor. He can't quite remember what the guy said he does for a living—something with investments, some kind of advisor or banker. Clearly he's loaded. The apartment has floor-to-ceiling windows and a Steinway. Stewart wishes he'd paid more attention when the guy told him his name. Tizak or Tazak, something with a z and a k. Stewart was too surprised to register what he actually said. Stewart had been checking him out from across the room for at least half an hour, until the banker disappeared in the crowd, then *bam!* he was right there, introducing himself.

He had a British accent. It threw Stewart off; he wasn't expecting him to sound like he'd gone to Oxford or Cambridge. He was ripped and had a leather band around his left bicep. Stewart wasn't sure what the band meant, but he felt himself growing aroused. "How come you're standing there all by yourself?" the banker asked, smiling. He had a killer smile. Stewart liked the contrast of his white teeth against the black skin of his face. Stewart imagined the man sticking his tongue deep in his mouth. He looked strong. He looked like he knew what he was doing.

Stewart fumbled for something to say. He felt himself turning red, though—thank God—it was too dark in the bar for the guy to see that. The man stuck out his hand, and this too made Stewart uncomfortable, because he hated shaking hands when his palms were sweaty. The banker's hand was warm and dry. He was out of Stewart's league. He could have scored with anyone in the bar.

The drink is strong, makes Stewart's mouth burn. It feels good. "What is it?" he asks.

"Rémy Martin XO," the banker says, putting his hand on Stewart's shoulder and giving it a squeeze. "You like it?"

Stewart nods, looks at the rows of small African carvings on the bookshelf next to the piano. "These are cool," he says. It's a stupid thing to say. He feels like an idiot calling what are probably valuable sculptures *cool*.

"The ones on this shelf are all from Nigeria," the guy says, pointing to the rhinoceros and the elephant and the lion. Nothing fazes him; he's a smooth operator. Stewart asks questions about the carvings, about Nigeria. The banker launches into a story about how his father was a diplomat, about growing up in a place called Victoria Island, about the beaches.

"Do you go back to visit? Do you miss it?"

"Hell no, I don't miss it. Do you know what people do to fags in Nigeria? Sissy boys get stoned to death. Does that sound like a good time? People there are ignorant. They still believe in sorcery and witchcraft and exorcisms."

Stewart remembers a documentary he saw about Pentecostal preachers in the Niger Delta, impassioned men who poured acid on kids whom they claimed were possessed by demons. He wonders whether he should bring the topic up, whether it will piss the guy off. "So your parents don't know you're gay?"

"Fuck no. My parents think I'm living with my girlfriend. They think I'm gonna get married. What are you, the KGB?" Stewart apologizes, and the guy picks up a jade dragon with bulging eyes. "This is my favorite," he says, handing it to Stewart. "It's from Indonesia. My father gave it to me when I graduated business school."

"What's his name—Grendel?" Stewart asks, trying to be funny. He wonders whether his breath is okay, wishes he'd brought mints.

"Relax, kiddo. Come on, take your shirt off, I'll give you a massage."

"Don't you want to get me drunk first?" Stewart asks. This too is a stupid thing to say, because the fact is he's already feeling light-headed.

"I don't need to get you drunk. You're not going anywhere."

Stewart says he needs to use the bathroom. The guy nods toward the hallway. "First door on the left."

Everything in the bathroom is marble—the countertops, the tiles and floor. White marble with tiny veins. Expensive marble. The drawers are practically empty. This is obviously just the guest bathroom. Stewart opens the cabinet and finds a travel-size tube of toothpaste that hasn't been used. He squeezes blue gel onto his finger and rubs it over his teeth and gums. Next to the toilet he sees a copy of the *Economist*. "Tazik Eze" reads the mailing label.

Stewart washes his hands and looks in the mirror. The light is soft, flattering; still, he thinks the shirt he's wearing is ugly. It's too tight, makes his arms look skinny. Three hours ago, when he was at home, getting dressed, he didn't think he'd actually hook up with someone. How many times has he gone to the Ramrod and stood alone in the corner, nursing a club soda or, sometimes, if he was feeling adventurous, a beer, until it was time to shuffle back to his apartment?

He almost stayed home tonight. He owes his mother a call. Last week he got a letter from her, blithely informing him that she'd just adopted a five-year-old girl from Russia. The news wasn't entirely surprising. For years Heike has been threatening to adopt this or that baby. "At least if I had myself a little Guatemalan girl, she would be grateful," Heike said, repeatedly. It wasn't until Heike told him about the girl in Lipetsk whose parents abandoned her at a police station as an infant that he wondered whether she might actually go through with the cockamamie idea. He knows Heike is probably mad at him for not having called to congratulate her, but he's too exhausted to deal with another headache right now. He just finished his first year teaching at the women's college in Boston where he got a job last fall, and he's running on empty.

When Stewart finally returns to the living room, Tazik is sitting on the couch, petting a huge mastiff. The dog is lying next to him, drooling. "Everything okay?"

"Yeah, sorry. I had a hangnail or something and I used your clippers to cut it off. I hope that doesn't gross you out too much?"

"Yeah, I'm totally grossed out. Come over here and let me take a look. Have you met Max? Max is my partner in crime."

At the couch, Tazik takes Stewart's hand and examines it. "Which finger?" Stewart shows him the thumb on his left hand, and Tazik kisses it. "Better?"

Something about Tazik makes Stewart feel like a little kid. He probably isn't that much older than Stewart, but he acts like he owns the world, like he belongs in the world.

Tazik isn't shy about taking off his clothes. He's tall, a few inches taller than Stewart, and it doesn't look like there's an ounce of fat on him. Stewart feels like a pip-squeak, standing in the same room. He throws his shirt on the armchair, and, as he's about to lie on the bed, Tazik grabs him and wrestles him to the ground. "Pants? You think you're going to get away with just taking off your top? We're not at the playground, girl."

Stewart isn't sure what to say. He doesn't want to take off his pants, not yet. Sometimes, if he gets lucky, if he hooks up with a guy he thinks is really hot, someone who's built like a brick shithouse, Stewart feels overcome by shame, by self-hatred. It's not just that he's thin. It's not just that he doesn't have muscles. It's more than that—it's the fact that his essence is slight, that his bones are like toothpicks, that everything about him is inconsequential.

Even his skin, his coloring, turns his stomach. He hates the fact that he has red hair, hates his freckles and skin that burns rather than tans. He wishes his hair were dark brown or black. Sometimes, if he stands in the bathroom at night with the light off and looks at himself, he imagines himself with dark skin. He hates the fact that sometimes, when he's in California with his mother, people make comments about how much they look alike, hates the fact they think Stewart's hair is just like his mother's, loathes the look his mother gives him at these moments: *See, don't think you're so special, you're just like me. You're mine. We're the same.*

"I saw you staring at me in the bar," Tazik says, nuzzling Stewart's ear. "You couldn't take your eyes off me. Isn't that right, kiddo. Am I your type? You like black guys? You liked to get fucked by black cock?" Stewart looks away. He's studied identity politics and race theory, knows what a cliché this whole situation is—the skinny white nerd getting turned on by the ripped black guy, the other.

The tape that Tazik uses isn't masking tape. At least Stewart doesn't think so. It feels more like the glossy packing tape you use to seal a box at the post office. Stewart isn't sure how much time has passed. He's on the bed now, his wrists fastened to the bedposts. This he was okay with. He doesn't remember resisting when Tazik took two lengths of nylon rope from the closet, or maybe the nightstand, and cinched them around Stewart's wrists. He remembers being turned on. It was part of the game, Stewart remembers. Tazik and Stewart were role-playing. Isn't that what it's called? Isn't this what Stewart wanted? Why else would he have gone to the Ramrod and stared at a guy in a muscle shirt with a leather strap around his left arm? Why else would he have gone back to this guy's place, no questions asked?

At least the guy isn't entirely grossed out by Stewart's body. At least he didn't laugh when Stewart finally disrobed. If anything, he became more insistent. Something seemed to come over him. His fancy pedigree went out the window. His Oxford manners evaporated. In the bedroom, he told Stewart to shut up. "Like this," he ordered, when he wanted a different position.

Stewart wonders whether something is wrong with his nipples. His left nipple in particular is aching now. Stewart tried to indicate that the guy was being too rough, but he didn't want to come right out and tell him to stop. He didn't want to draw boundaries unnecessarily. The last guy Stewart dated told him he had too many boundaries, that he was too rigid and restrained. Here he is, now, being relaxed.

Here he is about to get raped.

He wonders whether Tazik will at least use a condom. He wonders whether he'll end up with AIDS. Occasionally his mother sends him newspaper articles with photos of skinny men, men with no hair, lying in hospital beds, wasting away. *Be careful!* she writes in her notes. *Don't let anyone give you something you regret.*

Stewart feels at some remove during the events that take place. He feels the weight of Tazik's body on him, feels Tazik's force, but what happens on this king-size bed, in this high-rise condominium with a doorman and a sky deck on the thirtieth floor, seems to be happening to someone else. It's as if Stewart were floating above the bodies lying on the sheets, like a ghost or a deceased version of himself.

It is not rape. There is no force beyond that to which Stewart has, in some way, granted his consent. He doesn't want the man to stop what he's doing, doesn't want it to end.

He loves Tazik, wants to spend the rest of his life with Tazik. He likes his bearing, likes the fact that he grew up in Africa and moved to England at the age of seventeen, that he has bronze statues from Malaysia and Nigeria and Congo. He craves his lips and his penis, his masculinity. This is who Stewart wishes he could be. Someone whose palms do not sweat. Someone who drinks Rémy Martin XO. Someone who owns a mastiff.

"What did you say your name was? Stevie? Stacey? Is that it? Stacey? You look like a Stacey. My girlfriend in upper school was named Stacey. But her titties were bigger than yours. She actually had titties. What's wrong with you? Haven't your titties started to grow yet? What's the matter? Cat got your tongue? I'm just playing around with you, kiddo. It's okay. Don't get all pouty on me. We can cuddle if that's what you want. Is that what you like? To cuddle? Don't you like it when I talk dirty to you? I get it—you're the sensitive type, right? You want a man to caress you. Okay, then. How about this? Do you like this?"

Then later: "I bet you like to wear dresses. Do you wear dresses? Did your mommy put you in a little pink tutu this morning and drop you off at school with your lunch box? I bet you were a momma's boy when you were growing up. Is that what you were, a little momma's boy?"

In the background, Stewart recognizes the music of Erik Satie. Tazik Eze has put on Satie to make love to Stewart. It is like a gift for Tazik to have chosen that CD, something Stewart cherishes, chords and passages he's listened to many times on his own.

At first, the tape was part of the game. "I'm going to wrap you up and put you in a little suitcase and carry you with me everywhere. Wouldn't that be fun? To go everywhere together?"

Stewart wondered whether it was punishment for having been so tongue-tied earlier in the evening, so clumsy with his words. Sometimes, when the right topic comes up, Stewart can be a decent conversationalist. Sometimes, but not always.

Better not to be able to talk, actually. Better to have tape affixed to one's mouth.

And so when Max, the mastiff, started making sounds in the hallway outside of the bedroom, retching noises in the middle of the night, when Tazik jumped out of bed to check on his partner in crime, Stewart couldn't say, "Tazik, is everything all right?"

He couldn't say, "Let me help you, my love," when Tazik exploded at the dog, cursing about the vomit on the hardwood floors.

Or, "Honey, don't worry about it, come back to bed, I'll clean it up."

All he could do was lie with his face in the pillow, because he was on his stomach with his arms above him, fastened to the bedposts with the lengths of white rope, tape across his mouth. He strained to listen to what Tazik was doing out in the hallway. He listened to the running water and the tearing of paper towels and Max's whining, because the dog was feeling contrite. Poor fellow, Stewart thought. It isn't his fault. He didn't mean to get sick.

It was then, on the bed, facedown, that Stewart remembered how, when he was in third, fourth, fifth grade, visiting his father in Colorado during the summers, Raymond sometimes made him come outside and watch him load the gun he kept in a wooden chest that looked like it might have been owned by a sixteenth-century buccaneer. Raymond kept one pistol in the glove compartment of his car, in case there was trouble on the road, and one in the massive chest next to his bed, and sometimes he went outside to the dirt and the gravel and bushes, and pointed the gun at a target in the distance—a piece of paper with a bull's-eye emblazoned on it, nailed to a hulking wooden post—and pulled the trigger.

The sound was louder than anything Stewart had ever heard. It made his ears ring, made them go numb.

"Keep your eyes open now. Watch how I do this, kiddo. One day you may need to defend yourself. See how my finger pulls the trigger back gently. Look at me, son."

For some reason this is what lodges in Stewart's mind then, with his arms cinched to the posts: it is hot, the sun is high overhead, and there are flies everywhere. He remembers the heaviness of their bodies, their frenzied buzzing. Because they were frantic: trapped in Raymond's house, up against the windows, trying to get out. They were inside the house, and outside too, near the rattlesnake skin Raymond had hung from one of the wooden beams above the porch. The flies were delirious with the scent of rotting flesh, because sometimes, when Raymond was driving and he came across a rattlesnake on the road, he hit the brakes and took the shovel out of his trunk and went after the creature, Stewart sitting in the car, seatbelt still on, watching the scene unfold, afraid his father would be bitten, afraid the snake would be killed—Raymond going after the coiled-up reptile, the hissing rattler that Raymond lunged toward and taunted and hollered epithets at—*cocksucker* and *motherfucker* and *cocksucker* again— and then pounded with the shovel's blade, leaving the monstrous head with its fangs on the side of the road.

Stewart remembers Raymond coiling the snake's body up and carrying it back to the car, smiling, then handing it to him to hold on his lap, with a rag to stanch the blood where the head had been severed.

He remembers the weight of the reptile, still warm from the sun, its scales like a mosaic of scabs. He sat still in case the beast wasn't actually dead, knowing that when they arrived back at his father's house, Raymond would nail the snake to a beam, slit its body lengthwise with a hunting knife, peel the skin off, like cellophane from a grape Popsicle. He remembers Raymond cooking chunks of the snake's muscular body in an iron skillet and making Stewart eat the charred flesh, telling him it was a delicacy very few people would ever have the opportunity to taste. "No faces," he said as Stewart chewed.

What occupies Stewart's mind in this hermetically sealed apartment with central air are the flies and the snakeskin drying in the sun and the sound of the snakes' rattles, which Raymond gave to Stewart as a kind of souvenir, and the memory of the time when Raymond made him come outside and hold the gun in his sweating hands. Made him steady his breathing. Told him to look at the target in the distance, to stand up straight and throw back his shoulders and stop sniffling and, once and for all, to be a man.

Sometimes a thought takes hold of him and refuses to let go. Now, for example, while Tazik is in the hallway, Stewart worries that maybe he has cancer. Can one have cancer of the nipple? he wonders. A month ago he was at the doctor's office having a physical, and he saw the pamphlet in the waiting room: *Seven Warning Signs of Cancer*. The pamphlet talked about skin tags and lesions and moles with irregular borders. It described sores that didn't heal. It offered photos of a woman's arm with a horrible growth on it, something dark and grotesque that looked like it could never have taken root on a human being. Three black hairs sprouted from the monstrosity. The caption said the host was a forty-six-year-old woman who'd thought the growth was nothing to worry about—until it was too late and the malignant mass had sent cancer spores out into her body. Skin cancer travels under the surface of the skin, the brochure said. Removal of the mole, if one has waited too long, is of little use. Once the cancerous cells have spread, it is too late.

Stewart put the brochure back on the table in the waiting room, but afterwards, he wished he'd taken it with him. He wanted to study it. At home, he examined himself. He wondered whether certain freckles on his body had irregular borders. He made an appointment with a dermatologist. The first available opening wasn't until Tuesday, June 2, at 9 A.M.—three days from now. He imagines lying on his back in a white room with a high ceiling and fluorescent lights while a man in scrubs uses a scalpel to remove his nipples, first the right nipple, then the left. He pictures the man suturing the wounds—quickly, expertly—while a nurse waits at his side. She hands him scissors, then pads of gauze.

Stewart sees the surgeon above him and the snake on the gravel road, coiled and ready to strike, and his father sitting across from him—at the Stuckey's off the interstate—drawing two little rabbits on a napkin with a pen that the waitress gave him from the pocket of her dress. The rabbits have whiskers and cotton tails and big ears. "For Sandy," he writes beneath the drawing, smiling at Stewart. "You can bet your britches she's a Libra, kiddo. Do you see how graceful she is when she walks? Watch how she moves."

Stewart remembers the waitress folding the napkin, carefully, and putting it in the pocket of her dress, a blue dress that looks clean and freshly ironed, and she tells Raymond she's going to put it up on her fridge the minute she gets home, and she nods when he guesses her astrological sign, startled and amazed. "What time were you born?" Raymond asks. She shakes her head and says she doesn't know off the top of her head, but she can call her mom and ask. "I'll bet you have Virgo rising," Raymond says. "Get me the time, and I can do your chart. Have you ever had your chart done?"

In the hall, Stewart hears Tazik saying something he doesn't understand, and then: "It's okay, Maxy. It's okay, buddy. Just go back to sleep." Stewart pictures the dog's head resting on Tazik's lap while the man pets his belly. Stewart wonders whether he feels jealous of the dog then, resentful that it is the dog and not he who is receiving Tazik's affection. This is the thought that stays with him as he drifts into sleep.

When he awakes, the sun is streaming into the bedroom. The tape covering his mouth is gone, as is the rope that bound his wrists. Stewart is under a down comforter, and the bedroom is empty. His need to pee is ferocious. He gets out of bed, naked, and heads down the hall. "Hello?" he calls out. "Tazik?" He goes into the bathroom, the guest bathroom, and sits on the toilet. Sometimes he likes to sit down when he pees. It seems safer than standing up. No mistakes. He examines the veins in the marble.

He flushes the toilet and walks to the kitchen. Max is lying on his cushion, looking up at him. On the counter is a note:

Hey Stewart—
Went for a run. Donuts & juice in the fridge. Last night was
fun. Call me—560–7781
T

He wonders whether Tazik has really left the apartment, or whether perhaps he is hiding in one of the closets, watching him, testing him. "Tazik?" he calls again. "Are you here?"

He walks down the hall to a room with a glass desk and more windows overlooking the harbor. The desk is meticulous—a single document next to the computer, a Cross pen, nothing in the wastepaper basket, no piles of magazines, no newspapers. He sees a photo in a silver frame of Tazik and a guy with blond hair, both wearing parkas and goggles, on a snow-covered mountain. In the photo, Tazik's hair is longer, and he's wearing horn-rimmed glasses, and Stewart wonders whether the guy is Tazik's boyfriend. Perhaps it is someone Tazik used to date, because as far as Stewart can tell, Tazik is now single. Stewart saw only one toothbrush in Tazik's bathroom, one set of towels. Much could be interpolated from this photograph, were one prone to interpolation—Tazik pines for his ex, Tazik's heart was broken—but what purpose would such ruminations serve? So what if Tazik is single?

Bookshelves line the walls: Eliot, Keats, Longfellow. There must be a hundred volumes of poetry alone. Then fiction: *Ulysses, A Portrait of the Artist as a Young Man*, the works of Saramago. The books are arranged alphabetically. Behind a glass case, he sees a display of rocks: malachite and azurite and turquoise, beryl and tourmaline.

When Stewart was a boy, his father sometimes took him to a store in Denver that sold rocks and minerals, and bought him geodes and pieces of pyrite and agate and garnets. Once, after a heavy rain, they drove to Cripple Creek and looked for pieces of turquoise on the roads that were covered with gravel from the mines. After a few hours of combing the roadsides, Stewart had found just a few tiny pieces, but Raymond had found a large stone, larger than the pit of a nectarine. Stewart still remembers the moment: Raymond's disbelief as he bent down to pry the rock from the ground, his fingers working the dirt off its surface to reveal the full extent of the blue. Stewart wanted desperately to hold the treasure, to touch it, but he held back, not wanting to appear jealous or covetous.

Four weeks later, at the airport, Raymond took the rock out of his pocket. It was wrapped in white cloth, a handkerchief, and he handed it to Stewart as a gift. Raymond had been uncharacteristically quiet on their drive up to Denver. The waitress from Stuckey's, Sandy, had just broken up with him, and he'd spent the entire night on the phone trying to convince her to change her mind. Stewart, who still slept on the mattress under the printing press, kept his eyes shut, pretending to be asleep, but he heard everything: Raymond's pleading, his apologies and recriminations, the expletives when he slammed down the phone. He heard Raymond say he had no reason to live if she left him, then heard him go into the bathroom and sob.

Stewart opens the display case's sliding glass door and takes out one of the pieces of turquoise. It is larger than the piece his father gave him, and Stewart wishes, more than anything then, that it belonged to him. He wonders whether Tazik would miss it. There must be at least thirty specimens in the display case. The turquoise Stewart is holding is not the largest, not the most beautiful. He knows he will not see Tazik again. Tazik doesn't have Stewart's phone number, doesn't know where he lives. He doesn't even know his last name. Would it be so terrible if he put the rock in the pocket of his jacket and took it with him? To Tazik, the rock means nothing. Tazik has a Rolex and a stove that probably cost ten thousand dollars. Tazik has more of everything than Stewart will ever have. Stewart could take this rock, could get a Hefty bag and take all of the rocks. He could steal Tazik's collection of CDs and his books and his silverware—his cutlery—and Tazik would probably not miss any of it.

He considers his options. He could go into Tazik's kitchen and open an expensive bottle of red wine from France, and pour the contents onto Tazik's hand-woven rug. In some ways, the options are limitless. The apartment is quiet and outside is the ocean.

Stewart doesn't take the turquoise or the gold pen. He doesn't urinate on Tazik's mattress or smear fecal matter on his refined couch. Stewart isn't a child; he's not petulant. Instead, what he takes, after he puts on his clothes, is a single page from the journal he finds in Tazik's desk—the diary bound in soft calfskin whose pages are covered in tiny, meticulous prose.

The last entry, from just three days ago, is quite short, but for some reason it fills Stewart with a certain buoyancy:

> K isn't returning my calls. Called 3x over weekend, once yes-terday. Am I supposed to come back groveling, on hands and knees? Fuck him. How many times am I supposed to apolo-gize—for what even do I owe him an apology? He's the one who moved away to fucking Barcelona, and I'm supposed to be celibate while he thinks about things? Dr. Levy says I'm being dogmatic again. Fuck him too. Tells me he thinks I have an-ger issues I need to work through, as if I'm the only one who's angry. Suggesting we add another session on Tu AM—NFW! Am thinking of boxing up K's crap and sending it back to him UPS. Why shd I be his storage concierge?

This is the page Stewart rips free from the journal and folds into quarters. For a moment, he considers taking the entire jour-nal, but he's not that kind of person. He's eminently reasonable.

Stewart leaves Tazik's note on the kitchen table, untouched, and tucks the folded page into his pocket as he leaves the apart-ment, adrenaline coursing through his chest and his arms. He's not afraid. He's excited. He feels, right now, more alive—more powerful—than he's felt in some time.

1997

Potty
Mouth

Laurie knows it was a mistake to agree to take care of the dog, not that Roxy is a bad dog per se. Roxy is fine; it's Heike.

Heike convinced Al to go on a cruise to Norway and Sweden —at his expense, mind you—for two weeks. Then, being that the cruise was supposedly an *adult-only* affair, Heike twisted some poor family's arm to take care of the girl, Galina. Because Laurie had enough backbone, for once, to say no to that request. But here she is on a Saturday morning, her day off, stuck in the very situation she tried to avoid all along: having to go over and pick Galina up from the house of someone she's never met, three days after she drove Heike and her dad to the airport, because the girl is acting up and because Heike told the family that if there was an emergency they could call Laurie.

Laurie didn't give her permission for that. She agreed to house-sit with Crystal over at her father's place and take care of Roxy. She didn't agree to watch Galina too.

Laurie has her own problems: an ex-husband who doesn't pay child support, a boss with a stick up her ass the size of a baseball bat, a credit card balance of over $8,000—some of it from when Rob was out of work, before the divorce. She has a full plate. She does not need to be driving to a house on the other side of town to pick up a one-armed Russian child.

Heike isn't a Christian. She pretends to be Christian when it suits her, on Christmas and Easter and other select times when there's something in it for her.

Laurie is sick of it. What if she hadn't picked up the phone when it rang last night? What if she herself had been out of town on a cruise? Hadn't she promised Crystal the two of them would go to SeaWorld this summer? What if they were down there when Donna Nielson called, frantic, telling Laurie that Galina was throwing tantrums and getting in fights with the other children?

That's the kind of girl Galina is: a girl who fights with people. In the three years since she got to this country, since Heike went over to Russia for God knows what reason to adopt her, she's managed to make Crystal, a child who loves everyone and everything, *hate her guts*. How do you get a girl who is by nature happy and caring, who still believes in Santa Claus at the age of twelve, to hate your guts?

By pulling her hair, by threatening to pull the arms off her dolls, by putting one of Crystal's favorite rings inside her you-know-what. "Mommy, you just went past a stop sign!" Crystal yells as Laurie speeds through an intersection.

"Sorry, sweetie." Laurie's hands grip the steering wheel tight. She's all riled up inside. Now, on top of everything, she has to go to the bathroom. She's going to have to ask a stranger whether she can use their bathroom. "Mommy's just having a bad day," she says, taking a deep breath like the article she read at the doctor's office advised her to do.

"It'll be okay, Mommy. It's only for eleven days. Maybe Galina will be nice. Maybe we can all make cookies together."

Apparently Galina was trying to get the five-year-old to say dirty words to his older sister. Donna Nielson isn't shy about telling Laurie the details. She takes Laurie into the kitchen and explains that Danny, a boy with freckles and curly hair, came into Zoë's room when Zoë was putting on her shorts and very matter-of-factly told her to *go fuck herself*. Galina was hiding in the hallway, cracking up. Danny had no idea what was going on, and Zoë herself wasn't sure what her brother had said, but Donna, who was folding laundry in the pantry, heard it quite clearly. She demanded an explanation, at which point Danny started to cry. Eventually Galina confessed, but not without first telling Donna she smelled like vagina.

Galina remained unrepentant. Even after Mr. Nielson got home from work and took her into his study for a touch-base, she still insisted she didn't have to listen to him. "You're not my parents," she kept saying. "My parents are dead. My parents were killed in a fire."

"We feel for her, we really do," Donna Nielson says to Laurie now, leaning on the kitchen counter, a rectangle of sunlight coming in through the window. "We'd like to help out, but this is just too much for us."

"I completely understand," Laurie says. "She's a troubled girl. Heike should never have gone off like this and left her with you. I told her she had no business adopting a girl like that—a girl from over there, with a disability or what have you. I said my dad and her, both of them, were too old."

Laurie wants to be compassionate. She really does. She knows that's what being a Christian is all about. None of it is Galina's fault: being born with that deformed arm of hers, having her parents die in a fire or give her up for adoption or whatever the story was, having Heike swoop in to play Mother Teresa for a few months until she got bored and wanted to spend more time on her violin or tennis or whatever else caught her fancy. She was like one of those nervous birds that hop around in your yard, chasing flashes of sunlight reflecting off bits of chrome or glitter or what have you.

Laurie gathers up Galina's things and stands by the door, holding the girl's hand. "Now Galina, you say thank you to Mrs. Nielson," she says.

Galina stands there, expressionless. Laurie can't tell if the girl is sad or angry or embarrassed, like she should be.

"Tell her thank you, honey."

"I hate you all," Galina shrieks, yanking away. "I wish you were dead!" She throws the front door open and runs down the street. Laurie watches her skinny body, dressed in a red-and-white warm-up suit—the sleeve of the left arm flapping around in the air—take off with remarkable speed. Laurie hurries outside, trying to catch up to the girl, though she knows it's a lost cause. She's too out of shape to keep up, much less close the distance, and she just ends up jogging, out of breath, past the parked cars and nicely trimmed lawns, until she sees Galina stop and look back.

It takes Laurie and Donna and Mr. Nielson a good twenty minutes to get Galina to come out of the bushes where she's hiding. By then, she's got dirt on her face and she's crying hard. "I'm not getting in your stinky car, Laurie! I hate you," she wails. But Laurie, who's a nurse and is used to dealing with difficult patients, switches into nurse mode and takes hold of Galina's arm—her good arm—and gives it a squeeze, an adult squeeze. "Look here, Missy, I'm not taking your crap today. Do you understand me? You might be able to pull this shit with Heike, but not with me. You are going to shut up, and you are going to behave. *Comprende?*"

Five hours later, sitting on the couch with her feet up on the coffee table, watching *Law & Order*, Laurie knows she shouldn't have used that kind of language with a nine-year-old girl, but the bottom line is it worked. Galina got the message. She got in the backseat of Laurie's car, and, the whole way home, she kept her mouth shut. In fact, she kept her mouth shut for the rest of the day. She went into her room, refusing to come out for dinner— which was fine with Laurie, because it had been a long day, and what she really wanted to do was have a glass of her dad's Chablis and a piece of the German cake Heike had left for her and Crystal to eat.

The deal they'd made before the cruise was the following: Laurie and Crystal were supposed to walk Roxy twice a day, and, if it was nice outside, they would let Roxy lie on the grass after Laurie got off work and picked Crystal up from school. In exchange, her father would give her $200. Two hundred dollars wasn't a lot of money, but it would cover their food for the two weeks and that was something. If it had been up to him, her father probably would have given her more, but of course Heike had gotten involved in the discussion and had given her opinion, which was that Laurie and Crystal should be *happy to stay in such a nice house*, given how cramped and dark their apartment was.

"These little chores are nothing; they take ten minutes a day," were, as Laurie recalls, Heike's exact words.

Her father is a good and reasonable man. How he ended up with such a ballbuster baffles her. "I don't have a good feeling about her," Laurie said when Al told her about the arrangement he and Heike had come to regarding the house. Somehow, her father had fallen in love with Heike, or so he claimed, and wanted to marry her. He was still grieving Laurie's mom's death and wasn't think-ing straight. They were all still grieving. *Are* all still grieving. Having your mother die at the age of sixty-three as she's picking up non-dairy creamer from the grocery store, having a truck full of used tires driven by an illegal alien slam into her Volkswagen at forty-five miles per hour in a 30 m.p.h. zone is not something one quote unquote *gets over*.

That stays with you. It affects pretty much everything you do for the rest of your life. That's how Laurie rationalizes her dad's decision to fall head over heels in love with what Laurie some-times refers to as—excuse her French—a bitch on wheels. He was acting out of grief.

The arrangement Heike proposed to her father made it clear, as far as Laurie was concerned, what kind of person Heike was: she wouldn't marry Al, because if she did she'd lose her prior husband's pension and social security benefits, but she would live with him. More specifically, she would buy his house from him—*their house*, the house Laurie had grown up in—and move in and charge him rent. She would give him $245,000, a good $50,000 less than the place was worth, and he would pay her $700 a month in rent, plus utilities. That was the arrangement she pro-posed, and that was the arrangement he accepted. It didn't seem to bother him one bit. In fact, when Laurie told him she thought it was outrageous, that Heike was taking advantage of him, Al shut her down.

"I'm not discussing it, Laurie. Heike and I are moving in together. Heike's buying the house."

Of course Heike was thrilled with the way things played out: she sold the place she'd been living in for well over $300,000, pocketed the difference, and ended up with what she told everyone was her dream home, the house with the best view in the Vista del Mar complex—a view of the golf course and beyond that the Santa Ynez Mountains. The whole thing makes Laurie sick to her stomach.

Two days before Heike and her father are scheduled to get back from the cruise, the phone rings. It's a Friday night, and Laurie has gotten some videos from Blockbuster for the girls to watch. Crystal wanted *The Little Mermaid* and Galina wanted *The Lion King*, and since it was only a dollar extra to get both, Laurie decided to splurge.

Laurie lets the answering machine pick up, and she's only paying half attention to the caller's voice when she realizes that it's Rob. He's leaving her a message about tomorrow, Saturday, the day he normally spends with Crystal. "I'm real sorry, but something's come up. I've gotta go out of town for a few days—"

"Rob?" she says, picking up. "What's going on? Did something happen?"

Getting to keep Crystal to herself tomorrow, not having to drive over and drop her off at ten in the morning, is fine with her, but something about the message smells fishy. Rob has a certain sound in his voice that Laurie has learned over the years means he's lying.

"Oh, hey, Laurie," he says. "No, nothing's wrong. I just need to drive up to Fresno to do a job."

"Up to Fresno? You're gonna drive up to Fresno for a job? What kind of job?"

Rob is a terrible liar. That was why she figured out he'd been sleeping with her best friend, Darlene; it was why she found out his contracting business was going bankrupt while he was out losing three hundred bucks a night playing poker.

Rob hems and haws and ends up spilling the beans: he can't see his daughter tomorrow because he's driving to Vegas with Kimberly, a waitress he met a few months ago, to get married.

"You're fucking kidding me," Laurie says, feeling free to make her language as colorful as she wants, since she's taken the cordless out to the garden. "Tell me you're kidding."

"I'm sorry, Laurie. I have to."

"What? You got her knocked up?"

How long had it taken her to get to the bottom of things—two minutes? Three, tops? Rob was an idiot. He was a thirty-nine-year-old man who hadn't learned to put a condom on his dick. "That's just great. Surfer Rob strikes again," she says, hanging up on him. She opens the sliding glass door and sees the girls still sitting in front of the TV, mesmerized by the image of a lion talking to a monkey with a stick.

"Kids, I'm going out for a little walk, okay? Will you guys be okay?"

"Sure, Mom," Crystal says, barely looking away from the screen.

Laurie walks around the side of the house, out to the street. She walks past the other houses in the complex, many of which she spent time in at one point or another as she was growing up. She walks past the Walkers' house, which is now owned by an Indian family, and the Echeverrías' house, whose daughter, Pamela, was Laurie's best friend through junior high and high school. None of her friends from school live here anymore. Most of them have gotten married and moved away. A few people have gotten divorced, but amazingly most have stayed married. The few she stays in touch with seem genuinely happy.

Next month, she'll be turning forty-one. That sounds really old to her. When she was younger, she imagined that by the time she was forty, even thirty, she'd be happily married and have kids—at least three. Growing up, she'd always wanted to have a big family. She didn't think that she'd have a hard time conceiving. She didn't think her husband would end up falling in love with her best friend.

Now, here she is raising Crystal on her own. Which is fine, except that she's starting to wonder whether she'll ever meet someone again. Heike always gives her a hard time about her weight. She makes jabs about the food Laurie eats, about Laurie's thighs. Two weeks ago, Heike had a little birthday party for Crystal over at the pool, with party favors and whatnot. Laurie didn't want to go, but Crystal likes Heike. She wanted to go swimming. So they went, and the whole time Heike kept trying to get Laurie to put on her bathing suit. "Come on Laurie, put on your bikini," Heike kept saying. "It's such a nice day." Heike looked like a candy cane in her striped two-piece. Laurie felt like smacking her.

It wasn't that Heike was trying to be mean; sometimes she's just completely oblivious. Like the time a few months ago when she tried to set Laurie up with a guy from Trinidad, someone named Octavio, who works as a janitor at the courthouse. "What's wrong with him?" Heike kept asking.

"I don't know," Laurie said. "He's just not my type."

"What do you mean? He's a very nice man. He's very reliable. He's hard working. He has a good heart. What's not to like? Is it because he's black?"

"No, it's not because he's black, Heike. What—are you saying I'm racist?"

"Not at all, I just don't understand."

At the time, Laurie didn't know what it was about Octavio that she didn't like. Maybe he just wasn't the kind of guy she pictured herself with. Sometimes, she wonders whether she might still be in love with Rob.

I need to move on, she thinks, stopping at the end of a cul-de-sac that leads out to an expansive field, lined with huge eucalyptus trees that sometimes, in the early morning, have crows in them. She remembers getting up early when she was in high school and going running out here, cutting across the field and following the trail at the end of the bluff down to the beach. Sometimes she'd run six-plus miles. She looks up at the sky, which is bright and clear and full of stars. Maybe when Heike gets back, I'll tell her to have Octavio give me a call, she decides. She hears a plane flying overhead, then looks at her watch and sees she's been gone longer than she intended. She wonders if the girls are okay.

She's just a few blocks away when she realizes that the commotion she hears—the sound of a dog barking and, in the background, harried voices—is coming from the vicinity of the house. Up ahead, she sees flashing lights. She picks up her pace.

Sure enough, as she comes around the corner, a pair of fire trucks are parked in front of her dad's driveway. The trucks are monstrous. They look like something out of a movie: two hulking beasts of silver-and-red metal that barely fit on the street. There are people everywhere—neighbors and policemen and firefighters in full firefighter regalia. One of the firemen is crouched on the front lawn, next to Crystal, who is bawling her eyes out. Laurie runs over and hugs her, and two of the men explain that everything is okay. It was just a fire in the oven: some paper bags caught on fire accidentally and no one was hurt. "I'm sorry, Mommy," Crystal keeps repeating between sobs.

Laurie can't keep track of the feelings going through her—shock, terror, anger. "Whose idea was this?" she yells. "Was it Galina's? Who turned on the oven?"

Crystal can barely make eye contact with her mother. She tries to explain how they found some frozen cookie dough in the freezer and wanted to make cookies as a surprise.

"You decided to make cookies as a surprise?"

"We didn't know there was anything in the oven. We thought it would be okay."

Laurie asks where Galina is and then sees her over by the big elm tree, egging Roxy on. Roxy is going crazy, barking at the neighbor's cat, which is up in the branches, its fur raised, staring down. Laurie has never seen Roxy so excited. "Galina, you come over here right now and tell me what happened!"

Galina doesn't budge. She looks at Laurie, then looks back at the cat. "Get him, Roxy!" she shouts. *"Here kitty,"* she screams, making a kissing sound.

Even after a neighbor—someone Laurie hasn't ever met, with house shoes that are supposed to look like bunnies—comes over and swats Roxy, trying to shut her up, Galina keeps standing there looking up at the cat, as if she thought it might sprout wings or shoot bolts of lightning out its claws. Apparently, Heike had decided to store grocery bags in the oven. It had to have been Heike's idea. Laurie's father would never have done something that inane.

One of the firemen tells Laurie she's lucky they got there in time. He tells her she really shouldn't be leaving her two girls alone in the house like she did. "I know, sir. I'm sorry," she says. She decides not to tell him that only one of the girls is her daughter. She has no interest in being lectured right now. He's still talking to her when she leads Crystal back inside. The kitchen is full of smoke, and Laurie opens the windows to start airing the place out. After that, she'll have to get out the broom and dustpan and get the ashes out of the oven. Then she'll turn the TV off and put the girls to bed.

Three weeks later—after Heike has called Laurie in tears at 5 A.M., from Oslo, to tell her that Al had a heart attack and had to be flown by helicopter from the ship to the hospital; after her father spent eight days in intensive care; after Laurie and the girls drove down to LAX to pick them up, Heike pushing Al down the long corridor at the airport in a wheelchair, her father looking pale and weak, but, considering the circumstances, better than Laurie expected; after Laurie and Crystal went back to their apartment and adopted the neighbor's cat, a tabby with orange paws and white whiskers—Laurie finds herself eating pork chops and mashed potatoes and a green vegetable she's never had before, something bitter that sticks in her teeth, at a place called the Pirate's Cove with Octavio from Trinidad. He has a gold necklace around his neck, with a cross, and he tells her he likes the way she laughs. They share something called *panna cotta* for dessert, and he asks her whether she wants to go for a walk down by the harbor to look at the ocean, and, because Crystal is spending the night at her father's place, and because tomorrow is Sunday and it doesn't matter what time she gets up, she decides, without much hesitation at all, to say yes.

1999

Driving
North

Five years ago, when his mother announced that she was flying to Moscow to adopt a five-year-old girl, Stewart did his best not to react. His mother had always been the kind of person who made threats, who cajoled and coerced, until she got her way. For years, she'd been threatening to adopt one of the children she sponsored in Mexico and Guatemala and Romania, to bring a child home to live with her in Ventana Beach, so she would have someone in her life who loved her, who appreciated her.

According to his mother, Stewart was an ungrateful son. He was ungrateful and unloving, and his decision to move to the East Coast had been a slap in the face.

And what had Heike done to deserve such an ornery child? Why should she grow old alone in California and die, leaving her savings to him, when she could adopt one of the cute little girls whose photos she'd seen in the magazines and newsletters and Christmas cards she received from abroad? After everything she had endured in this country, wasn't she entitled to a little happiness?

"Be my guest," Stewart said.

He didn't use those exact words of course. He told his mother he loved her and was sorry she felt lonely. He expressed concern for her well-being, asking whether she was sure she could, at the age of fifty-eight, really take care of a child, a girl whose left arm was essentially missing—whether she was willing to make the sacrifices this decision would require, because he knew that despite the fact that Heike insisted her life was miserable, she did like her trips to Germany and Acapulco and the cruises she went on with Al.

"What sacrifices?" Heike replied. "It will be fun. This little girl is an angel. They sent me a video from the orphanage showing her singing and dancing. She enchanted everyone in the room."

When Stewart asked her what Al thought of the plan, she had an answer for that too. "Don't always worry so much what others think. I am your mother. Think about my happiness for a change."

And so Heike went to the bank and withdrew $5,000 in twenty-dollar bills and got on a plane from Los Angeles to London and then on to Russia and adopted herself a blonde girl. Had the child turned out to be happy and grateful, had she been the least bit appreciative and loving, everything would have been marvelous, but Galina wasn't what Heike had in mind.

She didn't like the little dolls Heike bought for her, the dolls that came from Leipzig and wore dirndls and *walkjankers* and whose eyes opened and closed. She didn't like Heike's good German cooking. She wanted Pop-Tarts for breakfast. She preferred Chuck E. Cheese's pizza with pineapple to rouladen and dumplings and sauerkraut with gravy made from scratch. She wasn't grateful at all, and Heike was miserable, even more miserable than before, and now she was saying that the whole adoption had been a mistake.

Stewart kept his mouth shut—on the phone when she told him how Galina had gotten suspended from school for calling one of the boys in her class a "beaner," and in person when his mother picked him up from the airport for his Christmas vacation. Because she still called his visits to her house a vacation.

In the car, on the way from LAX to Ventana Beach, Heike gave him an earful about Al's incontinence, about the fact that, just four nights ago, they had to stop when they were driving home from the movies so he could use the bathroom at Wendy's, about how she had to use the sink in the men's bathroom to wash out his underwear, and about Zhana Smolenski, the Russian woman whom Heike had initially referred to as a godsend—because the Smolenskis had two children whom Galina adored and because they invited Galina to spend the night sometimes so Heike and Al could have a few moments of peace and quiet.

Apparently, things with the Smolenskis had begun to unravel recently. Heike and Al had gone to Aruba to use a timeshare that was about to expire, and Galina had stayed with the Smolenskis, and when Heike drove over to pick the girl up, Galina refused to get in the car. She cried and said she'd rather die than go back to that stinky place. Heike had brought Galina a little wind-up dog that played music and turned somersaults, but Galina didn't even look at the dog. She swiped it away with her arm, her good arm, and said, "I hate you, Heike."

And had the Smolenskis tried to help? Of course not; Zhana Smolenski had probably poisoned the girl against her. "The woman is impossible," Heike said in the car, on the 101 North, the freeway that was taking Stewart farther and farther away from his life in Boston, from his home, from civilization. "Two weeks ago she calls me up and tells me I'm not a fit mother. Can you imagine? She has a PhD in mathematics and takes a very haughty tone with me."

The whole way up, sitting next to his mother in her little Toyota, Stewart tried to look like he was paying attention, but all he could think was that he'd made a colossal mistake—that letting Heike talk him into staying until New Year's, letting her talk him into not renting a car, allowing himself to step into the web she'd woven for him was not just a mistake, but a miscalculation of potentially disastrous proportions for which he could blame no one but himself. Could he risk telling Heike how he really felt? Could he say Mrs. Smolenski was right, that Heike was in over her head, that Galina would be better off living in a different household? Not unless he wanted his head chewed off at the neck.

He felt sorry for Galina; he did. He knew what she was going through, what it was like to be raised by someone like Heike. And to some extent he *had* tried to be there for her. He'd bought her presents along the way, had played Stratego with her, and Old Maid, but he was not going to give up his life for her.

He was not going to give up everything he'd worked for to come back and play peacemaker, to assume the role of big brother to Galina and consigliere to Heike, or whatever it was they expected of him. That was not going to happen. He'd barely made it out in one piece himself. The situation was quicksand.

A sound, not quite human, wakes him in the middle of the night. It takes him a moment to remember where he is; he wonders whether the neighbor's Doberman has caught a skunk or raccoon, but then he realizes the sound wasn't made by an animal. He gets out of bed, pulls on his pants, and hurries to the kitchen, where Heike is down on her knees, in her nightgown, holding a hammer. On the carpet a rat writhes in pain, its head and chest stuck to a glue pad. "Look at this poor thing," she says, handing him the hammer. "It's in agony. You have to smash into its skull." There are dark circles under her eyes, and her hair—gray at the roots, and orange elsewhere from attempts to restore its natural color—is frizzy and untamed. "Don't just stand there!" she shouts.

"You want me to kill it?"

"We have to—there's no alternative."

"I thought the exterminator said the rats were all gone."

"Ach, the exterminator is for the birds. All they do is send me huge bills. Look—the rats are still here!"

"Can't we just throw it away or something?"

"Throw it away? This thing is *alive*. Don't you see how it suffers?"

"Jesus," he says, taking the hammer. "Maybe we should try to drown it instead."

"Fine. You always choose the easy way out." She picks up the glue pad, rat and all. The rodent's hind legs strain to gain traction.

Its tail is long and dark, like a snake crossing asphalt. As they head to the bathroom, they pass the Christmas tree in the living room, and Heike tells Stewart to unplug the lights. "I asked Al to do it before going to bed. Does he listen? Of course not. Everything falls on my shoulders."

He bends to unplug the lights; it's the same tree they've had since he was in high school—the tree he and his mother and Gerry purchased on sale at May Company and fastened with bungee cords to the roof of their car two decades ago. The gifts, nearly all for Galina, are wrapped in the paper Heike recycles year after year—green and white sheets with gold bells and mistletoe and candy canes with pieces of leftover Scotch Tape.

In the bathroom, Heike shoves the glue pad into the toilet, submerging as much of the rat as she can. Stewart tries not to look, but he can see one of its legs moving, its tail flapping. The bathroom has a ripe smell, the smell of accidents that have accumulated over time, never properly cleaned, always covered with air freshener. Something pungent and citrus.

The tail stops thrashing, and Al appears in the doorway. "What's going on?" he asks, groggy. He's tall and thin, his pajamas two sizes too large.

"Nothing," Heike says. "Just go back to bed."

"You need help?" he asks, fingering his hearing aid.

"No, I don't need help. Go to sleep before Galina wakes up and starts getting rambunctious." Heike tosses the rat—mouth open, teeth protruding obscenely—into the wastepaper basket.

This is the image that stays with Stewart when he goes back to bed. It's 4:00 A.M., 7:00 in Boston, the time he normally goes to the gym. He lies awake, looking at the popcorn ceiling, illuminated by the garish Santa Claus the neighbors display in their yard every year. He examines the cobweb in the corner of the room, scrutinizing the desiccated insects suspended above him, looking for movement. The pillow beneath his head is lumpy and stained. He wonders if it's the same pillow Gerry used during his final months, when he went through round after round of chemotherapy, Heike nursing him day and night, putting compresses on his forehead to bring down the fevers, while Stewart stayed holed up in the library, three thousand miles away, writing a dissertation on T. S. Eliot.

He wonders how long it will be before Al ends up bedridden. The first few years he and Heike were together, he made an effort to hold his own, but the last few times Stewart's visited, he's seemed more and more out of it. It's gotten to the point where he can't stand up to Heike at all, can't defend himself from her badgering and criticism and bulldozing. His mother preys on this kind of weakness. Galina herself, who initially treated Al like a father figure, calling him papa and sitting on his lap at night when they watched TV, has started acting like he doesn't even exist.

Stewart wakes to the sound of rain; even though it's already 9:30, the sky is lead gray. Heike's collection of dolls sits on the dresser, staring at him. Their eyes, all blue, are always open these days. One of the figures, a girl with braided blond hair, is missing her eyelashes—one of Galina's earliest acts of defiance when Heike refused to buy her a toy gun she wanted at Kmart. Stewart dresses and goes to the living room, where Galina is on the carpet—in her favorite orange sweatshirt, the left sleeve flapping at her side— watching cartoons.

"Heike!" she calls out. "Stewart's awake." Without pausing, she asks who he thinks is stronger: Superman or Wolverine.

"Wow, that's a tough one, Galina. I don't know."

"Wolverine, of course. Superman doesn't even exist."

"And Wolverine does?"

"You finally got up," Heike says, walking into the living room with a dishrag in her hands. "I was worried something had happened." She glares at Galina. "Your brother is here. Turn that thing off so we can spend some time together as a family."

"But I'm in the middle of a show!" Galina hollers, grabbing her knees with her good arm and rolling back and forth. Stewart goes into the kitchen, where Heike is mixing batter in a large bowl, and sees several of the glue traps piled up in a plastic bag on the counter. "You're throwing those away?"

"I have to. I can't go through last night again. So what if these rats eat through the carpet."

"Where's Al?"

"He went to the store. Someone ate all my almond slivers. Must have been Galina. She better watch it or she'll end up fat."

Stewart pours some cereal and eats at the counter while Heike enumerates the people she still has to bake stollen for—Bernie Kramer, the man she plays tennis with on Wednesday mornings; Galina's teacher, Mrs. Castañeda; Lois, a neighbor who sometimes plays violin with Heike and who takes care of Roxy when Heike and Al go to Las Vegas; the Smolenskis.

"The Smolenskis?" Stewart says. "I thought you hate them."

"Hate them? I don't hate them; I need to keep them on my good side." Stewart watches his mother knead the dough with her hands. She's wearing a fitted red jacket, something short and shiny that looks like imitation leather, like something Michael Jackson might wear. He considers asking where she got it, but what's on his mind now isn't his mother's wardrobe, or the Smolenskis, or the number of stollen that still need to be made. What's on his mind is the fact that today is December 22 and he's scheduled to stay in California until January 2 and that once he gets home he will have just eighteen days until spring semester starts: eighteen days to prepare for the three courses he'll be teaching and to finish an article he was supposed to have completed two weeks ago. Eighteen days to digest a substantial body of secondary literature on the relationship between violence and the grotesque in the work of Flannery O'Connor and to come up with a compelling argument, a *groundbreaking* thesis, that will shed new light on the theme of disfigurement in the work of one of his favorite writers. Because if he does not finish this article before classes start and receive an acceptance from a decent journal in the next few months, he might as well kiss his shot at getting tenure goodbye.

Because the chair of his department told him, in no uncertain terms, that he must publish at least three more pieces in the next eighteen months if he wants any hope of getting enough votes. Stewart knows the deal: he's heard stories about promising academics, rising stars, who failed to get tenure and whose careers never recovered—who ended up adjuncting for three thousand dollars a class at third- or fourth-tier schools. At community colleges in Kansas.

He could have spent the entire day obsessing about the precariousness of his professional future and about the unreasonable demands being made on his time by his department and his students and his mother, had Roxy not lumbered into the kitchen. He's still sitting at the counter nodding and smiling when his mother lets out a shriek. "Who let this dog in here? Out, out, out!"

Heike has dough on her hands, but that doesn't matter. She grabs Roxy by the collar and pulls her toward the front door. "Look at this carpet! Who did this? Do you see how muddy her paws are? Al, did you let Roxy in from the garden?" She opens the door, pushes Roxy outside, and slams the door.

"*Mom*," Stewart yells as Roxy lets out a yelp. "You just slammed the door on her tail!"

He rushes over, opens the door, and guides Roxy through the hallway and into the garage. She walks slowly, her legs stiff. He tries not to look too closely at her fur, which is thinning near the tail, exposing scaly flesh. He can't remember the last time he took Roxy for a walk. For the past several years, whenever he's come home to visit, he's avoided her. Occasionally he'll pet her, but only if he's certain he'll be able to wash his hands right away.

In the garage, he takes a rag and wipes off her paws, one by one. She looks at him, her eyes milky with cataracts. Her tongue moves in and out of her mouth, slowly, as if she were trying to swallow something lodged in her throat. Her nails are long, the pads of her feet cracked. He holds his breath, moving as quickly as possible.

Hour after hour, it rains. Stewart had hoped to go running, but how is he going to run in this weather? How is he going to get out of the house when he doesn't have a rental car? He could borrow his mother's car, but what if he has an accident? The last thing he wants is to be responsible for something happening to her car. What he wants to do is go into his room, the room Heike calls his room, despite the fact that he hasn't lived at home for nearly two decades, and get some work done, because it makes no sense for him to stand in his mother's kitchen listening to the endless bickering—over what should be eaten for lunch, and whether crumbs are falling on the sofa chair, and whether Galina will please come into the kitchen and decorate the Christmas cookies that Heike baked for her.

"Come in here please or you don't get any stollen. *Now*."

"I don't want stollen. I hate stollen!"

"You hate stollen? Since when do you hate stollen? You told me you loved my stollen. Al, can you please discipline her?"

But Al's hearing aid is not turned on properly, and he's watching a show about the Amazonian rainforest, where a man is explaining it rains more than 240 days a year, rains so much that moss can grow at the rate of up to eight millimeters per month.

Stewart needs to take a deep breath, to remember that what goes on in this house is not his life, no matter what his mother says. He needs to not feel implicated when Galina does finally come into the kitchen and, instead of sprinkling the red sparkling sugar crystals on Heike's snowmen and reindeer, showers them onto the sticky surface of the two glue pads his mother left on the counter. He needs to not intervene when his mother yells at Galina and says if Galina doesn't shape up, Heike will send her back to Russia once and for all.

Just twenty-four hours ago, he was a well-adjusted, thirty-six-year-old adult, an assistant professor of English literature at an up-and-coming women's college in Boston, a scholar of twentieth-century poetry and prose. And now what is he? A reclusive adolescent barricading himself in his room, giving himself pep talks, telling himself that his mother is crazy and he's already done everything he can to intervene, that soon enough he'll be back in his one-bedroom condo with his books and his notes and his porn.

Mechanical pencil in hand, Stewart tries to read an article arguing that the self-mutilation Hazel Motes inflicts on himself at the end of *Wise Blood* is not an effort to find redemption, but he can't concentrate. He can spend days, weeks, ruminating over the implications of O'Connor's decision to maim and blind and kill her characters, can debate the nuances of physical versus emotional impairment in her work, yet when it comes to the person who is now his sister, to the people who are his family, he does his best to eradicate them from his mind. Maybe he is selfish. Instead of sitting in his room feeling sorry for himself, he should be spending time with Galina. He should take her to the mall or the botanical garden. After the adoption, the first few times Stewart came home to visit, Galina greeted him enthusiastically, rushing to give him a hug, going on and on about her favorite TV shows and arcane facts she'd learned about the Soviet empire. Whenever they went to a restaurant, she insisted on sitting next to him. This time, however, she's been more distant. It's probably just as well, he decides.

The sound of Galina's TV amplifies. *"That's it,"* Heike screams. "I said no more TV. Go to sleep!"

"Just ten more minutes!" Galina hollers back.

He hears some kind of scuffle, then a banging sound as his mother cries out. Stewart gets up and opens his door. "What's going on? What happened?"

Heike is sitting on the floor of Galina's room, rubbing her arm. "I can't take it anymore! I'm too old for this. Look," she says, raising her elbow. "This child is a monster! I try to take the remote, but she yanks it away. I'm no match for her. Tomorrow you go to the Smolenskis. Do you hear me? I could have broken something! Do you want me to end up in the hospital? *Is that what you want?"*

Galina is sitting on her bed, staring at the TV. Heike bursts into tears and pushes past Stewart, slamming the bathroom door. Stewart tells her she's overreacting, but she doesn't respond. He walks back to Galina's room, where she's twisting a piece of green yarn around the tip of her left arm, which ends with a small appendage that looks like a partially formed finger. It's covered in scar tissue, as if it were disfigured in some kind of fire. Heike insists that Galina's arm was this way at birth, but Stewart wonders whether maybe something happened at the orphanage when she was an infant.

"Come on, Galina. I think you better turn that off now."

Galina continues to stare at the TV, refusing to look up. "You're not my boss." She lets go of the yarn and brushes her right hand against the back of her head, where her hair is so short it's bristly. This too was a source of conflict.

Stewart returns to his room. When he finally falls asleep, his dreams are fleeting. He wakes up feeling something crawl across his left arm. He rubs the skin, trying to kill whatever was there, then pulls up the sleeve of his sweatshirt to see whether anything bit him. It's still dark outside, but he can tell the rain has stopped. All he hears is the sound of a frog. He gets up, puts on his running pants, and opens the door, holding his breath.

Roxy lifts her head and looks up at him. In this position— reclined, head lifted—she looks like a sea lion, her body corpulent from years of too many leftovers: half-eaten bowls of cereal, sour-cream sauces, week-old mashed potatoes and gravy left at the back of the fridge. For years, Roxy has eaten Heike's cooking grate-fully. No wonder her fur stinks, Stewart thinks. He heads toward the garage to put on his running shoes, and Roxy gets up and lumbers over. Her tail wags stiffly. Her nose is dry, the whiskers around her snout gray. "Good dog," he says.

He finishes tying his shoes, then heads out the garage and up the street. He crosses the mesa behind his mother's house, hear-ing the crows call to one another in the eucalyptus trees at the far edge of the fields. He makes his way down the trail to the ocean and begins traversing the shoreline.

It's still early when he returns to the house, but everyone is up. Al is sitting in the armchair in the living room, wearing sun-glasses, eating cottage cheese with apricots, and drinking tomato juice. Galina is in her room watching the History Channel, and Heike is in the master bedroom, ominously quiet, packing a suit-case laid out on the bed.

"Good morning!" Stewart calls out, like a department store greeter.

"Yes, good morning," Heike says morosely; she doesn't turn to face him, but he can tell she's been crying.

"What's going on?"

"Our little girl is moving out."

Stewart crosses to the other side of Heike's bed and sees that her eyes are puffy. In the sunlight, her skin looks grotesque—he can see faint scars under her ears, areas where the skin is taut in some places, bunched up in others. The coloring is uneven. Bit by bit, he coaxes the story out of her: this morning, before Heike had even woken up, Galina called the Smolenskis and told them Heike finally agreed to let her move out. Apparently, when Heike blurted out that Galina should go to the Smolenskis, Galina took the statement at face value. The Smolenskis agreed to come over and pick her up the next day at 2:00.

"She's going to move out? What do you mean? For good?"

"You heard me, the girl hates it here. She despises me. You've seen how she behaves."

"Yeah, but that doesn't mean she should just move out. They said they want to adopt her?"

"Ach, I don't know. Don't get so technical with me. She said they invite her over there for the week. It's the same thing. She might as well be there with them. It's what she wants."

"Did you talk to them?"

"Why are you asking me all these questions? No, I didn't talk to them. *You* call them if you care so much. You come here for a few days and think everything is so easy!"

Stewart has to circle the lot three times before he sees a white minivan backing out of its space. The driver is halfway out of the spot when he stops and gets out to open the trunk. "Why don't you get the tickets while I deal with this joker," Stewart tells Galina. She's peppering him with an endless stream of questions when she pauses for a moment, takes the money, then dashes across the street. A movie about machines that sedate humans to extract their energy isn't something he'd normally see, but this outing isn't about him. "Talk to her, Stewart," Heike had implored. "She'll listen to you."

The fact is he has no idea what he's supposed to do. On the one hand, his mother said she's sick of Galina, wants to be rid of her once and for all. On the other hand, Heike pleaded with him to convince Galina to change her mind. After the movie, they go to Baskin-Robbins, followed by the bookstore. "Stewart," Galina says when they're looking at the books on military history, "do you think Hitler was really as bad as everyone says?"

Stewart studies her face.

"I'm serious. Do you realize he was one of the most effective leaders in history?"

"He also killed millions of people."

"True, but he did it because he was trying to make his country stronger and more powerful."

Stewart wonders whether she understands what she's saying. "Galina, do you know how many Russians Hitler killed? Do you realize that he sent disabled people to gas chambers?"

"So?"

"So—doesn't that bother you? Wouldn't it bother you if someone said anyone who walks with a limp or has a mole on their left cheek should be killed?"

"No. If I was living then, I would think he should kill me too. My arm is totally deformed."

He crouches down and puts his hand on her shoulder. *"Time out.* I know that life has sucked for you during the past few years, but you are way too smart to think that." Stewart tells her that when he was her age, he hated his life, that he couldn't wait to move away, but as soon as he got to college, everything changed. He takes out a napkin from his pocket and wipes the smudge of chocolate off her chin.

"It's okay, Stewart. You don't have to try to make me feel better. It's really not that big a deal."

"Yes, it is a big deal," he says, but Galina isn't listening to him anymore. She's turned her attention to the Christmas card boxes stacked atop one another on the nearest display table. She's been shifting one of the boxes at the base of the arrangement with her hand, and Stewart hasn't wanted to say anything, but he sees now that she's leaning against the boxes. As he registers this, as he's about to take control of the situation, the boxes tumble to the ground, twenty or thirty of them.

"Galina!"

She turns and dashes out of the store at full speed. Stewart starts to pick up a few of the boxes, then stops and runs after her. He leaves the store, sees her halfway across the parking lot, and sprints as fast as he can, calling her name. It's dark outside, and though the parking lot is well lit, he's worried a driver might not see her weaving between the parked cars and the people looking for parking places. She's surprisingly fast, but eventually she stops, in front of Costco, and turns around.

"I'm sorry, Stewart. I know I'm a bitch." They're both breathing hard.

"You're not a bitch, Galina. You're dealing with a lot of shit. I get it."

They sit down on the edge of one of the planters and Galina tells him she doesn't think she can make it until college living with Heike. She doesn't think she can make it just a few more years or even months. "I know she wants you to convince me to not go to the Smolenskis, but why does she even care? She says like every day how adopting me was a mistake and she wishes she could just send me back to Russia."

Galina lays out her case, explains why he should drop her off at the Smolenskis on the way home. She promises that once Heike stops freaking out, she'll move back in and do her best to be nice. She says that right now she really just wants to see the Smolenskis' daughter, Natalia. She tells Stewart how nice Mrs. Smolenski is and how fun it is at their house, and twenty minutes later Stewart is giving her a hug in front of a large home decorated with Christmas lights that blink on and off, and he's watching his sister ring the doorbell of the kind of place he wishes he'd grown up in. He sees the front door open and a girl who is about Galina's age jump up and down and scream with excitement.

Stewart drives back to his mother's place, slowly, not sure how he's going to explain himself. When he arrives, the house is dark, and he parks Al's car on the street. He turns off the engine and sits quietly, bracing himself for what's next.

He walks along the flagstones to the front door and turns the knob. Inside, the house is almost completely dark. "Hello?" he calls out. He hears nothing except the sound of the TV. Al is sitting in the living room in his robe, drinking a glass of wine and watching a figure skating competition. Bathed in the glow of the TV, he looks like a phantom.

"Where's Heike?" Stewart asks.

"She's not here now," he says, holding out an envelope. "She left you a note."

"What do you mean?"

"You know how she gets. These things make her upset."

Stewart takes the envelope and opens the letter.

To my dear son:

I know it will surprise you to see that I am no longer at home when you return from your movie. I thank you for being so kind to spend the evening with your sister on your own, when I know your time is so precious. Hopefully you can make up for it by returning to your beloved Boston a few days earlier than planned. I know how important your work is for you, and for this I am thankful that you have found a good life for yourself.

The thought for me of spending another Christmas without Gerry, who I have realized is the only person who will ever actually love me, is too much to bear, especially when I am aware that it is such an imposition for you to fly here to be together with us. As you know, I had hoped that we would all have a nice time, but I am in no condition after Galina's announcement this morning to make Christmas Carols together and create a festive mood in the house.

I have decided to drive up north for a few days to visit Linda, the friend I told you about who lives with her sister Emily and their elderly mother. At least they will be kind to me. Their house is quite simple, but they have put up a tree and they are cooking a turkey which they say will be plenty for all of us to eat together on Christmas Eve. Please tell Galina that if she prefers to go to the Smolenskis I will not stand in her way. From the beginning I have known she does not love me. Perhaps I was foolish to believe that I could give her the life she deserves. I am an old woman now, and it is true she should have siblings her age. Please have her pack up her school work as well, since she has homework that is due when she goes back to class on the third. Maybe Mrs. Smolenski will be able to help her with these fractions they teach. For me, it has been many years since I did math problems like these.

In the fridge you will find plenty of jagdwurst, which needs to be eaten, though I know how picky you are. There is also red cabbage and pears from the farmer's market. Eat them if you like, or not, as you wish. I put no pressure on you.

For Christmas, I was going to give you $100 so you can buy yourself something you like, since I never seem to choose correctly. Here is a check, which you can use as you wish. Galina, as you know, has already opened most of her gifts. The package in green under the tree is the airplane she so desperately wanted. Tell her she can take it along and open it with her new family. The puzzle from K-Mart I will return.

Love from your,
Mom

"Is this a joke?" Stewart asks Al, who is futzing with the remote, trying to turn down the volume.

"She'll be okay. I think she just needs a break." He looks at Stewart and gives him a shrug.

"Are you kidding? She just decided to pack up and leave?"

"You know your mother. This is who she is. When you get to my age, life stops surprising you, Stewart. I lived with Deb for thirty-seven years, then one day a truck slams into her car. You think I'm going to get upset when Heike throws a temper tantrum?"

Stewart goes to Al's study, picks up the phone, and dials his mother's number. Her cell rings, then goes to voicemail. On his third try, she finally picks up.

"Mom! Are you all right?"

"Oh, Stewart, it's you. Yes, I'm fine."

"Where are you?"

"At Denny's. They have the most delicious Spanish omelets for just three-ninety-nine."

"I got your note. You sounded really upset."

"Upset? Why would I be upset? My little girl prefers the Smolenskis to me. My own flesh and blood despises me. It's okay. At least I know where I stand."

"Seriously?"

"What means seriously? You come home once a year if I'm lucky. You send me a card for my birthday and Mother's Day. You call a few times a month out of obligation. Is that love? When Gerry was dying of cancer, you were too busy to come home and spend time with us."

"Jesus Christ. Do you know how tired I am of all of your guilt trips?"

"Guilt trips! I do no such thing. Look, I'm not going to fight with you. Just go back to Boston. I know you have all these deadlines to meet. Have a nice Christmas."

Stewart hears her hang up. Part of him is relieved. He sits in Al's chair, looking at the photos on the wall of Al's first wife, and his children, standing together smiling; of Al when he was younger, building a sandcastle with one of his daughters; of Al and Heike in Hawaii, on their honeymoon. In the photos, Al looks happy.

In some ways, this outcome is better than anything he could have hoped for. Now he can fly home without feeling guilty. So what if there's a change fee. He'll be back in his own apartment. He'll be able to work on his article without being distracted.

His stomach feels light, the same feeling of adrenaline coursing through his system that he sometimes experiences before a date or a presentation. He doesn't want to be rash: he'll take a few minutes to weigh the pros and cons of each option. Before he calls Continental, he'll take a shower.

He goes to the bathroom and locks the door. He turns on the faucet and lets cold water run over his hands. He washes his face and looks at himself in the mirror—the light isn't flattering; it highlights the imperfections in his complexion, makes his teeth look discolored. He takes off his clothes and gets in the shower. He leaves the water on for a long time, thinking about the French toast his mother made for him the day before yesterday, which he left untouched, about the fight they had at the airport when she accused him of pulling away from her too quickly after she gave him a hug. He wonders what a good son would do in the current situation, what a good brother would do. Would he drive north in search of his mother? Would he move home to help raise Galina?

When Stewart finally leaves the bathroom, Al has gone to bed. He walks to the kitchen, takes a glass from the cupboard, and fills it with water. As he takes a drink, Roxy comes over to him, one step at a time. He reaches down to pet her, and immediately she lies down and rolls on her back, spreading her legs. Her skin is pink and gray; there's something bloated and unhealthy about its appearance. Her nipples are shriveled, barely visible. He sees a mass, something tumor-like, at the base of her ribcage. He touches her stomach, feels the warmth of her skin. He lies next to her on the carpet, in the darkness, resting his head on her body.

His mother is gone; he's free to leave. He says this to himself, again, as if testing each statement's veracity, probing its soundness. He should be happy, but, for some reason, it isn't happiness he feels.

Maybe she'll change her mind, he thinks. She's always been mercurial; maybe tomorrow she'll show up at the front door and they can open presents together, as they have every year for as long as he can remember. His mother will put on her dirndl and her lipstick. She'll comb her hair and put it up in a bun, and she will take the stollen out of the fridge and cut it into pieces and sprinkle powdered sugar on top. She'll arrange the pieces on her festive red-and-white platter and hand everyone a napkin, the good napkins she only takes out during the holidays.

The carpet in the kitchen is soft, and above him a stream of warm air wafts down from the vent. He wonders whether he might hear the rats gnawing inside the walls, and he listens, but the only thing he hears is the sound of the clock's second hand and of the heater. He likes it when the heater comes on. When he was a child, the heater's sound always made him feel safe.

He remembers how he and his mother used to sit in front of the heater together, after his parents' divorce, when they still lived in Colorado and it was cold. Often she told him stories about what it was like growing up in Germany during the war—how she spent afternoons in the woods collecting strawberries and blackberries and boysenberries for jam. She told him so many stories, some of which he still remembers.

2008

Iceberg

My dear, faraway Stewart,
    Tonight it is very cold, and I am sitting here freezing. Even
the robe you gave me two years ago is not warm enough. It is
not quite 4 A.M., but for me it is impossible to sleep. I just had
the most horrible dream.
    I was in Boston at a huge concert hall, surrounded by high
society. Women in their mink stoles and fur coats. Very fine
like my father sold in Germany before the bombs fell on us. I
had gone there to surprise you. It was the opening night of a
performance where you were the star, and I arrived late, despite
all my efforts. There I was, seated at the back of the theatre, when

suddenly everyone gave standing ovation. I stood up too, but then I noticed people staring at me as if to say *Pa! Who is she?* The woman to my left gave me the eye. I had no idea what on earth they were looking at, then the couple in front of me turned and snickered to one another. I looked down at my outfit, which I had brought along specially for the occasion, but it was not at all what I intended. It was just a tennis dress—a little nothing of a skirt and my training shoes with white laces. Somehow I had left my beautiful black gown in the subway or maybe the hotel room—I must have been staying in some kind of room somewhere, because I know how you are about wanting your privacy.

I was besides myself. Should I try to sit down and cover my legs? I wondered. Next thing I knew, the auditorium emptied out. People pushed past me to leave, but I could not go home. I hadn't even greeted you yet.

I walked toward the stage, but all the lights went off for the night and suddenly there was no one around. I called out your name and finally there came this gray-haired janitor shuzzling along with his broom. "Do you know where I can find my son?" I asked, but he had no idea who I was talking about. "Stewart Winter," I said, "I am his mother."

"Who?" he said to me. Apparently he barely spoke English.

I climbed up onto the stage, and he tried to push me back down with his broom, but by this point I was frantic. I toppled over him and felt his bony hands trying to grab me. Finally I made it past the huge velvet curtains, red as dried blood.

Then there came a well-dressed gentleman in suit and tie. "May I help you, Madam?" he inquired. He had one of these toothpick moustaches you see in the movies—very severe—and British accent. I told him I had flown in from California to see you. "But, Madame, Mr. Winter is unavailable, he does not take visitors without a guest pass."

This is when I woke up. It took me a while to orient myself and realize I was still in my bed, all alone.

Yes, I received the letter you mailed to me.

I have no idea how on earth to respond. You tell me all I care about is myself. You say the adoption of Galina was a selfish gesture, meant to manipulate you. Nothing could be further from the truth. I adopted the girl to give her a home. If she had stayed in Russia, she would have had nothing. The orphanage where she lived was terribly crowded and dirty. Once the children turn eighteen, they are kicked out to the streets to fend for themselves. I may not be a perfect mother in every respect, but surely the life she has here is better than what she would have had in this thirdclass city. Can you really be so cruel to hold this against me?

You say seeing me causes you tremendous anxiety. Why would this be? I have always done everything in my power to be a good mother to you. Yes, we struggled when you were young, but I did my best to give you a good childhood. Don't you remember how I put you on my lap and bounced you on my knees singing to you? I still remember the song vividly:

> Hoppe hoppe Reiter, wenn er fällt dann schreit er
> Fällt er in den Graben dann fressen ihn die Rabben
> Fällt er in den Sumpf
> Dann macht der Reiter PLUMPS!

On the word PLUMPS, I opened my legs and swooped you into the air and you laughed and said *Do it again, Mommy.*

The fact your father divorced me was no fault of mine. Do you think I chose to be a single mother having to take these part time jobs in order to make ends meet? Don't you think I would have liked to be one of these women with a nice house in Hidden Valley who had a charming husband and a big car?

You were probably too young to remember the struggles I had to go through. After the divorce, when we still lived in Colorado, I had to call your father and plead with him to take care of you on the weekend if I could not find a babysitter. He wanted nothing to do with you whatsoever.

"Stop calling so much," he scolded me. "I have no interest in this child. I hate babies."

He refused to change even your diaper. Everything fell on my shoulder. Without me, you would have had nothing.

Sure, we would all like life to be perfect, but this is not always the case. Think of what Galina has endured. Think of your own mother. What I went through as a child in war was just the nose of the iceberg. I must have told you how much I struggled when I first arrived in the United States with just a suitcase and a few dollars to my name. I had to learn everything from scratch— how to operate a washing machine, how to make an American breakfast, folding a man's shirts just so. The first family I worked for was Jewish and the wife ate nothing but black coffee and plain cottage cheese. Did I ever tell you about them?

I arrived there at night with bronchitis and hadn't eaten dinner. "Make yourself a soft-boiled egg," the woman said to me, and I had to ask the kids what to do. My English was still quite raw, and I had a hard time understanding what she said. Each kind of food had its own set of dishes, and she watched me like a hawk, making sure I didn't mix the silverware up. Every time I sinned against her, she grabbed the utensil out of my hand, putting it into the big flowerpot she kept on the ledge near her oversized windows. This was January, and I could see my breath on the glass in my room as I looked out over the garden.

The next weekend, the wife was having a dinner party and she asked me if I had a different outfit I could put on. "I'm so sorry," I apologized, "I have just this one."

"That's not appropriate," she said. "This is a dignified house. At least get yourself a proper brassiere."

Two days later, she caught her husband looking at me and she called me over to the pantry. "You're too slow for me," she said. "I need someone else." Back to the YWCA I went, crying myself to sleep.

A few days later I met a woman at the tennis court who told me about a family that was not very rich but needed someone to help them do household chores. The wife had left the husband and he was all alone with his kids and their grandmother, who was clinically blind. When I got to the house, I was again hungry. I guess it was late afternoon, but I hadn't eaten anything all day, and I saw a forlorn pork chop sitting in the pan with some rice.

The man of the house saw me looking at the pork chop and offered it. He let me sleep in a little chamber next to the kitchen with its own radio, and at night I listened to classical music from the telephone company, which brought performances from all over the world.

The family was nice to me and very patient. I thought things would work out, but one day I was bathing the grandmother in her tub and the phone rang. I went downstairs to answer the call and when I came back into the bathroom the old hag was bathing in her own blood. Apparently, she had tried to shampoo her own hair, and the bottle fell out of her hand, shattering. Of course, they said it was my fault.

These were tough times, yes, but then something happened that was for me even worse, something I have never told you before and which I will carry inside my conscience for the rest of my life. After your father divorced me and you and I moved to California, I felt very alone and was in need of someone who would be kind to me. I was a struggling woman with no friends or support and there came along one day a very debonair man by the name of Sam Cornish who took an interest in me.

He was a professor of biology at the university with kind eyes and what I thought was a good heart. I knew he was married, but he told me he no longer loved his wife and was planning a divorce. He said he found me desirable and wanted to leave her for me. I told him to wait until his divorce before getting fresh, but he always tried to lure me into his lab to show me these hairless mice he kept in a cage. Finally, one day, when you were at school, I allowed him to seduce me. He made love to me and from this one time, a little girl, a fetus, was conceived inside of me. Can you imagine? One single time. I had no idea what on earth I could do.

When I found out the news, I called Sam Cornish up and told him we had to meet.

"Not now, Heike," he said to me. "I'm on my way to a conference."

"Please," I said. "Something terrible has happened."

"Don't tell me you're in trouble."

"Yes, I am. I'm pregnant with your child."

"I can't talk about this now," he said, very cold.

"But you told me you loved me. You said you wanted to marry me."

"Nonsense. You'll have to have a procedure."

I stood there speechless in the kitchen, while you played with some little fuzzel on the carpet.

I had no idea what on earth I could do. I went to our next-door neighbor, a nice woman named Mrs. Herskovitch, who sometimes babysat you and broke down in tears. I told her everything. She was so kind to me. She took me to a doctor and lent me the money. The whole thing was terrible. I cried and cried, thinking about this little girl inside of me. I wanted so badly to keep her, but of course it was not possible. I was already too poor to take care of you.

Sometimes I wonder what kind of a person this daughter would have become. Maybe she would have learned the piano and we could have made music together. It happened so long ago, but I still think about her. Maybe I adopted Galina in part to make up for this. Is that so terrible of me to have done? You have made a nice life for yourself in Boston. You have a good job and friends. Now that Al is no more, I have very little. Please, Stewart, I beg you not to be angry with me. We each do the best that we can. Think about it.

With love from your,
Mutti

A
Kind of
Happiness

She takes turquoise pills—more than she should —to fall asleep. That and the wine usually allow her to make it until the alarm goes off, but today she wakes early, when the sun is just rising. She sits up in bed, letting her eyes adjust, looking out across the city, which, in the distance, resembles an illustration from a children's book, and, beyond that, the ocean. The view is the reason she and Yuri bought the house. "I could wake up to this for three hundred years and never get sick of it," he told her. "It's like looking out on eternity."

At least she still has the house.

She turns on the coffee maker, heads down the hall to Natalia's room, opens the shades. She still does this: closes her children's shades at night, opens them in the morning. She looks at Natalia's bed, her pillows, the posters of men in leather pants and platform shoes, singing onstage. The day before their trip to Lake Havasu, she and Natalia had a fight about one of this band's concerts. Natalia pleaded with Zhana to let her drive down to L.A. with a friend from school. "Seventeen is totally old enough!" Natalia shouted. "Jesus, Mom. Next year I'm going to be a senior!"

"Don't *Jesus* me, young lady," Zhana said, raising her voice, hoping Yuri would back her up. "I told you we'd talk about it on the trip. Okay? For now, though, the answer is no." Natalia had already broken her curfew three times that month, and Zhana felt she and Yuri needed to draw clear lines.

They were flying out the next morning. Yuri had just gotten his pilot's license, and he splurged and rented a plane, a Cessna 310 with six seats and barely enough room for the luggage. It was meant to be a family vacation, but there'd been an electrical failure at work, and Zhana needed to manually program a machine to finish the protein purification she was working on. "I'll catch a flight later on in the afternoon," she told them before she rushed off to the lab. "You guys can go waterskiing and I'll be there for dinner." It was the last thing she said to them. She got in the car and backed out of the driveway without even closing the trunk properly. Five hours later she was standing in line at the FedEx in the El Paseo Shopping Center, behind a kid whose iPod was turned up so high it sounded like he was carrying a boom box, when her phone rang.

"Mrs. Smolenski?" a woman said, butchering the pronunciation. "Is this Zhana Smolenski? Are you the wife of Yuri Smolenski?"

That was four years ago, give or take—three years, eleven months and nine days; now here she is in her bedroom, putting on a yellow pantsuit that's too tight in the hips and the thighs, looking at herself in the mirror, wishing she hadn't said yes.

When the invitation arrived two months earlier, she recognized Galina's handwriting right away; her penmanship—if it could be called that—had always been sloppy. The paper was cheap, the geometric pattern on the cover childlike. At the bottom was a quotation from Rabindranath Tagore, along with a reference to an "elegant vegetarian potluck." Galina and her fiancé, Adrian, were asking people to bring their favorite vegetarian entrée in lieu of a gift. The reply card had some kind of Hindu deity stamped on it, a figure sitting in the lotus position.

Zhana put the invitation and the reply card back in the envelope, telling herself she'd respond later, that she'd send Galina an email with a suitable excuse. She poured herself a glass of wine, put her feet up on Yuri's worn ottoman, looked through the rest of the mail: bills, pleas for donations to help children with cleft palates and animals in distress. She studied the ottoman—the woven fabric, fraying at the edges; the alternating red and black diamonds. (Can an ottoman belong to a person who is no longer living? she wondered. Perhaps instead of her husband's ottoman, the ottoman was now hers: *the widow's ottoman*.)

Zhana got up and went into the kitchen to get some crackers, and then, before sitting down again, she turned on the TV. She kept the volume off but allowed herself to watch the people on the screen. These people—smiling women leaning into the camera and holding products toward her, couples in kitchens and living rooms talking to one another animatedly, distinguished-looking men with ties, behind desks, discussing important events—had become her nighttime companions.

She finished the glass of wine and poured herself another. She looked at the invitation again and decided to tell Galina that she'd be away that weekend with her closest friend, Irina, celebrating Irina's birthday in San Francisco. Or maybe that she'd be out of the country on a business trip. That sounded better. She'd be in London for an all-hands meeting to discuss a new vaccine. Surely *that* sounded important enough. She'd send a nice present and wish Galina and her new husband the best of luck. Because the alternative was too much to bear. Because seeing Galina in a white dress with flowers in her hair would dredge up too many memories: of Natalia, of Matvey and Yuri. Of everything really. But especially of Natalia, because the date Galina had chosen— July 28—fell two days shy of what would have been Natalia's twenty-first birthday.

When they were younger, Natalia and Galina had been best friends. They were in the same class in school, two grades above Matvey. (Matvey: *Gift of God*. What gift? she thinks to herself now, looking into the mirror, putting on lipstick and rouge to hide her ashen complexion. What kind of God gives you a son, then takes him away?)

Back then, when the house was always noisy and Zhana couldn't wait to get home from work to help build a city out of Legos or a fort out of blankets and cardboard boxes, Galina came over frequently—for dinner and slumber parties and, a few times, water balloon fights. At first, Zhana thought nothing of it. She and Yuri always had their children's friends over. And one couldn't help but take pity on Galina. Her left arm disfigured at birth, raised in an orphanage in Lipetsk until the age of five, then adopted by Heike, a woman who seemed well-intentioned at first, but whom, ultimately, Zhana and Yuri could not stomach—a bulldozer, Yuri called her, a harridan who used people to her advantage.

It got to the point that they knew what to expect if they picked up the phone and heard Heike's voice: "Al and I are going to Vegas for a few days. Would you mind watching Galina while we're away?"

"You'll be here in October, right? Al takes me to Germany for vacation. He's never seen my hometown. It would mean so much to us. We'll pay for her food."

"I'm at my wits' end. This child is impossible. All she does is talk back to me. Won't you take her off our hands for the day?"

The answer, of course, was always yes. How could they say no? Heike was in over her head, too set in her ways to be a proper parent, too emotionally unstable. Her then-husband, Al, already well into his seventies, wanted nothing to do with the whole situation. Galina needed a proper family, craved the company of children her own age. Their house was big enough to let Galina stay over. Yuri had insisted on buying a place where, no matter how many kids or visitors they had, there'd always be room. Sometimes Heike offered them ten or fifteen dollars to help pay for Galina's food, but they never accepted. Not that they were wealthy, but they knew ten dollars meant more to Heike than it did to them. Heike was a stingy person: stingy with money, stingy with favors.

The one time Zhana had needed Heike's help, after the accident, when she herself was struggling to keep afloat, Heike hadn't come through. Irina had asked people to bring photos to the memorial service. Photos of the children, photos of Yuri. Heike must have had some; she'd had Natalia over for Galina's birthday on more than one occasion.

"You didn't have a picture or two?" Irina asked Heike when she arrived. It was raining, and Heike came wearing a red raincoat and white tennis shoes.

"Oh, my goodness, the photos. Yes, we have a few, but they're pasted into an album. I brought pie instead. I made a nice strawberry pie."

Irina recounted the conversation to Zhana word for word. Afterwards, when everyone had left, Zhana threw the pie into the trash.

Zhana hadn't even wanted to invite Heike, but she thought it was the right thing to do. By then, Natalia and Galina had fallen out of touch. Galina had dropped out of high school and moved down to Venice to live on the beach with a tribe of graffiti and performance artists. Occasionally, Zhana ran into Heike at Vons and they exchanged awkward sentences, Zhana always curious to know what Galina was up to but afraid to put Heike on the spot, afraid to seem too curious. She knew how touchy Heike could be. Heike had made that clear on numerous occasions over the years, calling Zhana up, accusing her of trying to steal her daughter.

Once, when she was eleven, Galina phoned Zhana, pleading with her to let her move in. "I hate it here. She's always yelling at me. Please let me stay there for a while." Heike showed up three days later, just after Christmas, in tears, pounding on the door, insisting that Galina pack up her things and get in the car. Natalia and Galina were out back, taping shopping bags together to make a mural, and Heike stormed through the house to the yard.

Three weeks after the invitation arrived, the phone rang. Zhana was in the bedroom, folding laundry, listening to Chopin's *Nocturnes*. She'd gotten home late from work and hadn't eaten dinner yet, because eating dinner alone was sometimes, still, too hard. She didn't recognize the number and picked up.

"Zhana? It's Galina! How are you?"

Zhana wasn't quite sure what to say. *I'm grand, Galina. Couldn't be better!*

"I'm getting married," Galina continued, filling the silence. "Did you get the invitation? I hope you can make it. It would mean so much to both Adrian and me. It's going to be really small—just thirty or forty people. Will you come?" She'd always spoken too quickly when she was nervous.

Zhana had had a few glasses of wine (because that was something she'd become quite proficient at, having wine on her own, sometimes an entire bottle in a single evening), and before she had time to formulate an excuse, she found herself admitting that, yes, she'd be in town. "Of course I'll be there. I'm so happy for you."

"I can't wait for you to meet Adrian. I think you'll really like him. I was afraid you might not come. I was afraid you were mad at me or something. I'm sorry I've been so out of touch."

There was a certain breathlessness in Galina's voice—the sound of a girl who'd fallen in love. She was still young, her life intact. Zhana kept the conversation light. The fact was she was happy Galina had called. Why rake her over the coals for not going to the funeral, for not even sending a note? It was all water under the bridge. Wasn't that the proper expression?

"I'm looking forward to seeing you again, Galina. It's been so long."

It wasn't until Zhana hung up—when she stubbed her toe on one of the bookshelves in the hallway that she herself had insisted, against Yuri's protestations, on having installed—that she burst into tears.

At what?

At the fact that she'd accidentally put a cotton blouse in the dryer? At the fact that Galina had been out of touch for almost five years and then expected Zhana to act like everything was okay?

One could spend one's entire life being careful—wearing seat belts, not allowing one's children to swim in the neighbor's pool without adult supervision, making sure the stove was always turned off, buying organic milk—but what good did it do when a bird, a Canada goose, happened to intersect with the path of a twin-engine monoplane headed on a sunny morning from Ventana Beach, California, to Lake Havasu? The papers called it bad luck. The plane should have been able to withstand a collision with a stray bird, but something went wrong, there'd been some kind of engine failure or technical malfunction. The local paper published a photo of Yuri, which Zhana herself had taken the previous year on a family trip to Yosemite. "Yuri Smolenski, 58, professor of anthropology," the caption read. Yuri was wearing a cap with a bear on it, a bear drinking a bottle of beer.

The botanical garden is nicer than she remembers. She hurries past the beds of roses and petunias and flowering bushes whose names she doesn't know, carrying a chickpea salad she picked up at the store, toward the music—a guy with a shaved head, dressed in some kind of green robe, playing a harmonium and chanting words Zhana doesn't understand—hoping she isn't too late. The ceremony has just started, it seems. The gathering is small: a hodgepodge of folding chairs and a few benches. She takes one of the seats at the back, next to an elderly man who's smoking a pipe. The man turns to her and smiles, wheezing a bit as he nods. Immediately, she wishes she'd chosen a different seat; she hates smokers, despises the feel of smoke in her lungs. At least there's a breeze. She crosses her legs, adjusts her left shoe. She hasn't worn these pumps for years. At home, when she put them on, they also felt tight. She wonders whether she's reached the age at which her feet have started to grow again.

She recognizes only a few people: Heike in the front row; a girl named Melissa who went to high school with Galina and Natalia (a girl Natalia hated because she tried to steal Natalia's first boyfriend); Heike's stepdaughter, Laurie—a vapid blond woman whom Zhana was forced to talk to last year at Al's funeral— sitting a few feet away. There's incense in the air. The pastor (is she a pastor?), a woman with lines of crimson paint on her nose, is wearing Birkenstocks and baggy pants that make her look like a genie. Galina has on a tie-dyed dress, and the groom, a tall, gangly man whose ear lobes have been stretched with huge piercings and whose nose has been skewered with some sort of miniature spear, is dressed in a toga. At least half of the people have shaved their heads, dyed their hair, tattooed their skin.

Zhana wonders how Heike took the news when Galina told her she was marrying Adrian. She wonders how she herself would have taken the news if Natalia had brought home someone who looked like he belonged in a circus. She knows what she would have done. She would have fallen on her knees and kissed the guy's feet.

Body piercings? Sure. *Facial tattoos?* Wonderful. *Dreadlocks?* Of course.

The guy could have been the Son of Sam, and that would have been fine with Zhana. "Test me," she wants to stand up and yell. "Make him my son-in-law. Make this my daughter's wedding."

At night, in bed, she sometimes wonders what she would give to have just one of her children back. She imagines herself talking to God, negotiating. Give me cancer, just let me have Matvey back for a day. Give me Alzheimer's, Parkinson's, Yellow Fever in exchange for breakfast with Natalia. Occasionally, when she's shaving her legs, she presses the blade into her shin, feels the bite of the razor. The blood doesn't bother her. She isn't afraid of death. If she had some kind of guarantee that there was an afterlife, if she knew that by dying she'd see her family again, would she be here today, sitting in the sun, watching another woman's daughter get married? Would she have gotten up this morning, taken a shower, combed her hair, squeezed her feet into these unforgiving shoes?

Occasionally time passes without her. She trips, stumbles, gets left behind. Now, for example, she finds herself in front of a plate heaped high with potato salad and kale and vegetable curry, wondering for a moment where she is, where the potato salad on her plate came from. The person next to her is telling her about getting evicted. It's Laurie, Heike's stepdaughter, whose eyeliner is always too thick. The one who complains—perpetually, it seems—about how tough it is to meet a guy.

Zhana doesn't know this person, not really. She doesn't care about Heike and Laurie and Laurie's daughter, Crystal, who wanted to come to the wedding but couldn't because she works as a nurse in the Phoenix area, where, Laurie tells Zhana, it is *much easier* to find a job.

"I'm happy for her," Laurie says. "She's done good for herself. What else could a mother ask for?"

Zhana could take the plate of potato salad and grind it into Laurie's face. She'd like to smear the mess into her hair. She's not interested in hearing about Laurie's daughter who recently bought a used Mazda. This is of no consequence to her. The fact is Zhana wants to be left alone. She wants to get up and leave these hippies with their nose rings and their harlequin outfits, the relatives from Paso Robles and Riverside with their weight problems and their boyfriend issues, and go home. She wants to lock the door, draw the drapes, pour herself a drink, and swallow a handful of rainbow-colored pills.

"Where's Stewart?" Zhana asks, changing the subject.

"Oh, God. Heike won't shut up about him. They had some big fight—you know him. Now he's refusing to talk to her or something."

Zhana perks up. She likes this. This is good. Heike's son isn't talking to his mother. This makes Zhana feel something—something other than sadness, a kind of happiness.

Galina rushes over and takes Zhana's hand. "Zhana, Zhana, I'm so happy you're here," she says, giving her a hug. She's wearing a necklace made out of red and white flowers. Her hair is a deep, vibrant blue, a shade or two darker than her eyes. She's smiling, radiant, happier than Zhana has seen her in years.

"Zhana, I need to ask you a favor. Could you say a few words? We're asking people to say something. Sort of like a toast. Is that okay?"

Zhana looks at the dimple in Galina's chin, the silver ring in her bottom lip. The girl who pierced her nose at the age of fifteen, who dyed her hair green at sixteen, whose parents left her outside an orphanage in one of Russia's dirtiest cities. The memories come back to her now—of Galina and Natalia giggling late into the night together, of Galina eating breakfast with them, sitting on the couch with them, eating popcorn, watching old movies.

"Of course, darling. I'd be honored."

"Thank you. I really appreciate it." She grasps Zhana's hand and squeezes. "I don't know how to say this, but I just want to tell you how sorry I am—about everything. I know I should have called you when it happened. I was a real shit. I was just—"

"Stop, Galina. It's okay."

"No, it's not. I was dealing with a lot of crap then. I let it get in the way." It looks like tears are forming in Galina's eyes. "I've really missed you, Zhana. Are you going to be around tomorrow? I want to come by your place so we can catch up."

Just then, a woman wearing a purple turban comes over and greets Galina, taking her hand and leading her away. They walk past the rose bushes to a shaded area under a eucalyptus tree, and the woman says something that makes Galina laugh. Sometimes

Zhana wonders what it would have been like if Galina had moved into their house. For a while, she and Yuri had discussed the idea, wondered whether they should broach the topic with Heike. It was clear Heike was struggling. Yuri thought she might have some kind of psychiatric condition. One moment she'd regale you with stories about men who tried to pick her up in line at Costco; the next she'd break down in tears.

Galina told them what Heike was like—how she yelled at Al day in and day out, about getting crumbs on the couch, walking too slowly when they went out for meals, letting the faucet drip. She told them that sometimes Heike and Al went off for the night without making dinner, leaving Galina at home.

In retrospect, Zhana realizes she probably should have gotten more involved. Though what could she have done? Called child services? Sued Heike for custody? On what grounds? That she was a bad mother? The world is full of bad parents.

People stand up to speak one by one. The man who played the guitar during the ceremony lights a stick of incense and begins chanting:

> Hare Krishna Hare Krishna
> Krishna Krishna Hare Hare
> Hare Rama Hare Rama
> Rama Rama Hare Hare

People join hands, repeating the invocation. Zhana sees Heike, three chairs from Galina, staring at the spectacle, a glum expression on her face. A woman with dreadlocks recounts the time she first met Galina. "I knew from the moment we spoke that we would be friends. She emanated light and understanding. She had a kind of aura that I'd never seen before. I felt when I was around her that I was in the presence of something transcendent."

A few minutes later, it's Zhana's turn. She stands and says that she met Galina through her daughter, Natalia, when Natalia was in fifth grade, that she'd immediately been drawn to Galina's charisma and energy, that she felt privileged to watch Galina grow up into a fine young lady, a lady whose life is full of possibility and hope. Zhana had told herself that she wasn't going to let things get maudlin, that she wouldn't go too deep, but here she is talking about the time that Galina came with them on a trip to Yosemite—the trip they took over spring break when Natalia was in seventh grade and Heike said she needed some peace and quiet. They rented an RV and drove up North together, Yuri and Zhana taking turns at the wheel, while the kids belted out "Sunday Bloody Sunday" and "Where the Streets Have No Name" and "Just Like Heaven." Natalia and Galina had entered the phase during which all they wore was black, and they pleaded with Zhana to let them use her eyeliner. "She and Natalia were inseparable," Zhana says, starting to choke up. "She felt like one of us, like one of my children."

"Yes, I know this fine young lady also," Heike interjects, suddenly, standing up. "I am her mother. I'm the one who brought her over here to this country. Without me she wouldn't be. Without me, there wouldn't be this wedding here today. *I paid for this all.*" Heike is wearing an orange dress, which shows off her cleavage. One of the straps of her bra is exposed—a black strap.

"Mom!" Galina shouts.

"What—am I not allowed to speak at my own daughter's wedding?"

"You said you didn't want to. I asked you—"

"Said I didn't want to?" Heike says, increasing her pitch. "I had no idea everyone gets up and shares their feelings this way. I had no idea you ask everyone to say something but me. I am your mother, after all, unless you forgot. I raised you!" People sit motionless, looking at Heike. Even the musicians have stopped.

"Heike," Adrian says, standing up and taking her arm. "Thank you. Thank you for sharing. We're all very grateful."

"Yes, I can see that," Heike continues. "I can see how grateful you are coming here in your T-shirts and gowns. What kind of wedding is this? Do you think God likes this kind of thing? Do you think he approves of these matches you light to make smoke?"

As Adrian tries to calm Heike down, Galina rushes away in tears, toward the parking lot.

"Galina!" Zhana calls out, hurrying after her.

"I knew it," Galina sobs. "I knew she'd try to ruin today! She promised me she'd bite her tongue for once. She promised."

"Please, Galina. Don't let it get to you. You know how she can be. It was a beautiful ceremony. It's a glorious day. Just come back and enjoy the rest of your lunch. We're all having a good time. Adrian is talking to her. I'm sure she'll be fine."

"Of course she'll be fine. *She's always fine.* What about me? What about Adrian? I knew she'd do this to us."

"Deep breath," Zhana says, giving her a hug. "You have to let it go."

The Christmas that Galina had spent with the Smolenskis— when Heike had a kind of nervous breakdown, driving off in the night to God-knows-where—had actually been one of their best Christmases ever. They bought Pictionary as a gift for Natalia, and everyone ended up spending hours drawing telephones and carrots and witches in trees, and drinking hot chocolate and eggnog, and then, prompted by the word *smore*, getting out the graham crackers and chocolate bars from the pantry and using a pitchfork from the garage to roast marshmallows.

When Heike knocked on the door, three days later—red-faced, bags under her eyes—she looked like hell. "Don't you have enough children of your own?" she shouted at Zhana. "Why steal Galina from me? *Why?*" Zhana tried to calm her down, told her no one was trying to steal Galina, but Heike wasn't in a state to be reasoned with. She barreled through the house, calling Galina's name, and then, when she found her in the garden with Natalia, pulled the girl through the house while Galina hollered: "I hate you, Heike! I wish you were dead!"

This morning, before she went to the store to buy the chickpea salad, Zhana went into Natalia's room to look for the charm Natalia bought Galina for her birthday when they were in eighth grade. The charm had the letters *Be— Fri—* inscribed on it. It was the companion portion of the Best Friends charm Natalia had saved her allowance to buy. Galina's had the remaining letters inscribed on it. The two halves fit together to form a heart. Each pendant hung from a necklace that Natalia and Galina wore around their necks—for years—day and night.

Zhana found the necklace in a box in Natalia's dresser, tucked between two layers of cotton. The charm is thin as a stamp. Zhana studied it, then placed it back in its box, and returned the box to the top drawer of Natalia's desk. Now, she wishes she'd brought it along. It might have cheered Galina up, though already her spirits seem to be lifting. Adrian has come over and taken her in his arms, and here he is rubbing her back, nuzzling her ear. Zhana feels out of place. Across the lawn, near a fountain, she sees Heike sitting on a bench, alone, looking at the water.

"I'm going to get myself another drink," Zhana says. Galina looks up at her and smiles and mouths the words *thank you*, reaching out to touch Zhana's shoulder. Zhana walks across the grass toward the woman in the orange dress—the dress that calls too much attention to itself, that shows too much sun-damaged skin—the woman whose last husband died eleven months ago and who now lives alone.

"Hi, there," Zhana says.

Heike looks up, surprised.

"How are you doing?" Zhana asks, almost awkwardly.

"Okay, I guess. Just watching these little ducks." Heike points to a family of mallards bathing in the fountain. "Look how happy they are playing together."

Zhana takes the spot on the bench next to Heike. "You know, you raised a fine young woman. You should be proud."

"What means proud? My daughter is like a stranger to me. I have nothing in common with her whatsoever. She might as well be from another planet."

"She's still young. Children evolve. Be patient." Zhana wonders if she should say more, if she should tell Heike that she should be grateful for the things she does have and stop feeling sorry for herself all the time. So her daughter turned out to be a bit of a rebel; at least she's alive. Zhana notices that Heike's stockings have a run in them and a hole in the toe.

Heike stands up and announces she's had enough and is going home. "They don't need me here. They won't even notice I've left. They're off dancing up a storm over there. Look at them."

Zhana has seen this side of Heike before—petulant, self-absorbed. "No, Heike, you should stay. This is your daughter's wedding." Zhana can see tears in Heike's eyes. "Sit down here with me. I want to talk to you."

Heike sits down again and gets a Kleenex from her handbag. "What is it? What do you want to talk about?"

"I want to clear the air. I know it's not my place to give you advice, but we've known each other a long time."

"I don't need advice," Heike says, crying now. "I'm fine."

"You're not fine. You're upset."

"Of course, I'm upset. You see how they treat me. I'm an afterthought here. Galina doesn't want me as a mother. I'm not the kind of parent she wants. She wishes she could have been part of your family, not mine."

"I know you think that, Heike, but lots of kids wish their parents were different. You think Natalia and I didn't have our issues? The night before she died, she and I had a fight. She wanted to go to a concert down in L.A. and I said no and she slammed her door in my face. How about that?"

Heike studies Zhana, then puts her hand on Zhana's knee. "I'm sorry. I had no idea." For a minute, they're both silent. They look at the grass and the fountain and the rows of rose bushes, then Heike says, "I was always so jealous of you. I always wished I could be more like you."

"I wasn't a perfect mother. I made my share of mistakes. Don't sell yourself short. You're the one who went over to Russia and adopted Galina. You're the one who picked her up from the orphanage."

"Yeah, but she never gives me any credit."

"Kids always take their parents for granted. She knows what you did for her. She knows you love her." In the sunlight, the ducks' feathers look iridescent and one of the ducklings is dunking its head in the water. "Come on," Zhana says. "Let's go join them."

Heike gives her a suspicious look. She blows her nose and looks at the people dancing on the grass in the sun—barefoot, dresses twirling, hair flying.

"It'll be fun," Zhana says, taking off her shoes. She reaches out and takes Heike's hand in her own. Heike's hand feels small. Zhana holds on tight, leading her from the fountain, around the rose bushes, over to the people who are twirling and clapping. The grass is cool on her feet. She leads Heike toward the woman with the tambourine and the man playing the drums and the sound of the sitar. Then she lifts her arm, still holding Heike's palm in her own, toward the sky. The sun is bright and she closes her eyes, focusing on the music, the rhythm and sound of the notes.

2013

Clear
Waters
Below

She thought the roads would have been busier today, the day before Thanksgiving. She'd braced herself for traffic, filled up the tank before she got on the freeway, thinking there wouldn't be another gas station for some time, but she realizes that was silly—every turnoff, it seems, has signs for fast food places and service stations and motels.

The woman she's visiting isn't an old friend. They've known each other for only a few months really, but when they met in San Luis Obispo, at an outdoor performance of Mahler's Symphony no. 6 in A Minor, they hit it off immediately. The woman, Casey Livingston or Livesy, had her dog along, a lovely springer spaniel she'd rescued from the pound. Heike took an immediate liking to the creature, and soon enough she found herself telling Casey her life story: the struggles of a single mother, raising a son on her own, and then, nineteen years ago, adopting another child. Both children were difficult, headstrong, fiercely independent, but Galina—so sure of herself, so defiant and outspoken—was nothing like Stewart.

Not that it mattered. At this point, neither one gave her the time of day, that much was certain. Both were off living their own lives. If anything, the girl was even more defiant than the boy, telling Heike to *fuck off* last year when Heike tried to pay her a visit—for Thanksgiving in fact. So many lines and boundaries here in America. Heike would never have had the nerve to tell her mother to *fuck off*. Omi would have slapped her.

"How dare you speak to me that way," Heike shot back on the phone, doing her best not to cry. "I am your mother!"

"I'm sorry, Heike. It's just not a good time. Okay? We're not doing Thanksgiving this year. I've got a show in January, and I'm under the gun."

"Yes, yes, I know. Your art comes first. I understand." She waited for an apology, a letter or a phone call, but none ever came.

Every so often, Heike looks down to make sure the dessert she's made—a strawberry pie packed with wonderful, ripe berries from the farmers' market—is still okay. She's placed it on the seat next to her, the passenger seat, and sure enough it's doing just fine. She wrapped it neatly in foil. A new piece of foil. It was the least she could do as Casey's guest. How nice it will be, she thinks, to spend Thanksgiving with a friend.

The thought of driving alone to Las Vegas to play the slot machines on her own, again, was too much to bear. Al wasn't much in terms of company, but at least when he was alive she didn't have to wait in line at the buffet by herself. She didn't have to sit in one of those booths alone, watching everyone else have fun. God, how she hates the holidays. Who knows, if she and Casey hit it off, maybe they can spend more time together. Casey is also single— older than Heike by at least five years, and a bit overweight, but functioning just fine. Heike wonders what kind of cook she is.

"We'll make a nice turkey dinner on our own, then," Casey had said on the phone. "Just us girls."

"Are you sure I can't bring something?"

"Just yourself, darling. Don't worry about a thing."

Casey hasn't ever been married, doesn't have children. "My pup is my boy," she said, leaning against the oak tree they found themselves sitting under, listening to the orchestra. And she was right. When push came to shove, weren't dogs always more reliable than people? You could raise a child, feed him, clothe him, give him love, sing lullabies all you wanted, but when he turned eighteen, none of that mattered, did it? The child would go off and lead his own life. His or her. Turns out boys and girls are the same. You'd be lucky if you got a card or a call. A visit: now that was asking too much. Too much pressure, too much *expectation*. There was a word Stewart liked. "You have too many expectations," he used to say, when he still talked to her. "You put too much pressure on people. You can't expect so much." Here in America, kids like to be free. People need their independence. No one wants to be tied down. No obligations.

Galina will be coming home for three days at Christmas. For that, Heike knows, she should be grateful. She'll bring down her sullen husband—Adrian, the electrician who chews with his mouth open—and her little girl, Amalia. Stewart will probably be off with that boyfriend of his in South America. Maybe he'll send her a postcard.

She could get hit by a car and end up bedridden and what would her kids do? Send flowers if she was lucky.

Halfway up the coast, Heike stops at a Taco Bell. She likes the Beefy Tostadas. That was always something she and Stewart could agree on. They both liked Taco Bell. Although the last few times he came to visit her, even that wasn't okay anymore. He'd started insisting that everything be organic. Organic lettuce. Organic tomatoes. Organic beans. Organic shampoo. Organic silverware. It had gotten to the point that she couldn't even give him a hug anymore. A kiss had always been too much for him. She got used to that. No kisses from Mom. That she could live with. But no hugs either.

And why? Because she was his mother, of course. Nothing she'd done had ever been good enough for him. Her clothes were always wrong. Her cooking was too greasy. She used too much butter and oil. Her ingredients weren't *organic*. And even if she did go out and buy organic things for him, it still wouldn't have been okay, because she'd touched it. He didn't want his food touched by human hands—at least not by *her* hands. If Luis touched his food, that was probably okay. Just not his mother.

At least Galina hadn't been picky about food, about germs. Galina would drop some toast on the carpet and eat it, no problem. She wouldn't clean up after herself, wouldn't wash her dishes, let her fingernails get black with dirt, but, hey, what can you expect? You can't have everything.

Heike tries to remember the last time she went up to visit Galina and that husband of hers, Benjamin. No, wait, Benjamin was her first boyfriend, the colored man she lived with down in Los Angeles. Adrian is her current boyfriend—husband. Could it have been five years since she went up to visit them? She tries to remember when they got married. It's 2013 now, she knows that much. She keeps a calendar in her purse, and she checked that this morning. Today is November 27, 2013. Yesterday, she went over to the rec center to play canasta. Canasta is on Tuesdays, so today must be Wednesday.

Sometimes, they give her extra sour cream, though not today. The woman at the counter, heavyset with freckled cheeks, is surly as can be. Not as nice as the Mexican fellow who works at the Taco Bell near her house. Not by a long shot.

She gets a small Coke too. Why not treat herself? She has the money. After all, she can't take it with her!

She sits at one of the tables with her food and sees a young girl across from her, nursing a baby. The girl can't be more than seventeen. She's drinking a Coke too, listening to her headphones. The baby looks like a newborn, it's so small. The girl is wearing sweat pants and a tank top, and though Heike can see a bit of her breast, the girl doesn't seem to care. "Watch out," Heike feels like shouting. "The kid will be out the door before you're done changing diapers. These are the good times. Enjoy them!"

Whatever Stewart says, she was a good mother. She did the best she could. If Stewart should be mad at anyone, it's Raymond. He was the one who wanted the divorce. He was the one who met someone else. There were plenty of times before he said *anything at all* that she was fed up, ready to leave, but she stayed. She stayed for Stewart.

Not that it matters now. "Dear Mother," Stewart wrote to her—When was it? Four years ago? Maybe five?—"I think it's best we cut off contact for a while. I feel too much anger to be in touch with you now. This isn't meant to hurt you; I just need my space."

She cried. She wrote letters to him. She tried to get Galina to intervene. Nothing helped. He needed *space*.

You can't change a person. That much she's learned. Stewart would sit in his room all day long with his nose in a book. Nothing she said or did could change that. Probably wasn't so bad in the end, given how Galina turned out. Up every night 'til two or three in the morning, even on school nights, coming home with alcohol on her breath, smelling up the house with the pot she smoked after school. Heike hadn't even known what the smell was at first—Galina had to tell her.

"It's pot, Heike! Marijuana. *Don't you know anything?*"

Galina didn't give a damn what anyone thought. She was fifteen years old, and she knew it all. She painted her nails black, dyed her hair purple, shaved her head. Anything to be different. Heike learned to go with the flow.

You want to go out and take drugs? Fine. You want to play hooky from school? Be my guest. Got suspended? Have a good time!

Galina wasn't going to be told what to do. When she was eleven, she moved in with that Russian family—until they got sick of her and kicked her out. Did Heike have to take her back? Of course not. She could have said: "Too bad, you made your own bed, kiddo." But that's not the kind of person Heike is. She welcomed Galina back with open arms. "Come to me, my daughter. Of course you can come home. So good to have you back."

In the parking lot, Heike reaches into her purse for her keys and can't find them. She rifles through her bag, sorting through the Kleenex and coins and scraps of paper and lipstick but comes up empty-handed. She rushes back into the restaurant and asks the woman behind the register whether she left her keys at the counter when she paid for her food. The woman couldn't care less. "Nope, no keys." That's all she says. Heike could be standing in front of her on fire, flames in her hair, and the cashier wouldn't lift a finger.

Heike searches her handbag again, then goes over to the table where she was sitting.

Nothing.

The tables all look the same: white countertops with orange trim. The only people eating now are some teenagers over in the corner, playing with their phones. She retraces her steps, goes back to the bathroom, then out to the car again, where, miraculously, she sees that she left her keys in the ignition. She opens the door, gets in the driver's seat, and says a little prayer, thanking God. She's not really religious, but sometimes she takes a moment to fold her hands together and close her eyes. She believes God exists. She believes there's a Heaven; you have to believe something.

Next to her, in the passenger seat, the pie is just where she left it. On the dashboard are the instructions she wrote out, painstakingly, telling her how to get to Casey's place. She checks her rearview mirror, then starts the car and backs up, slowly. She exits the parking lot, finds the right freeway entrance, the entrance to Highway 101 North, and gets back on the road to San Luis Obispo.

Casey's mobile home is smaller than she expected, smaller and more low-class. It's in a trailer park on the outskirts of town, a place where the roads aren't even paved. It's already dark when Heike arrives. The sound of crickets fills the night.

Her bladder is about to burst she has to go to the bathroom so badly. She hates to knock on the door and ask to use the toilet right away, but what can she do? She goes to the porch, rings the bell. Inside, she hears Ginger barking up a storm—the clacking of little nails on the linoleum.

"You made it!" Casey says, fumbling with the locks, then opening the door. "We were worried about you. Ginger thought you might have gotten lost, but no, here you are."

The place is run down. Worse than run down. The drapes are ripped, the carpet stained, the bathroom sink caked with grime. The toilet seat feels sticky on her buttocks and thighs. *My God,* she thinks, *what have I gotten myself into?*

Casey is sitting on the couch now, Ginger in her lap. "Are you thirsty, honey?" she asks. "Let mama up so she can get the lady something to drink," Casey says to the dog. The dog isn't what Heike remembers.

As Casey gets up, her robe opens a bit, and Heike sees that Casey isn't wearing anything underneath. Casey's stomach and breasts are all flab.

"Sit down, sit down. Make yourself at home."

The couch has a strange odor. Like something dead. Heike says she'll bring in her things, goes outside, takes a deep breath, clears the rancid scent from her lungs. She tries to calm down. This isn't what she had in mind, not by a long shot. Who is this person?

She gets her bag and the pie and goes back inside. Casey oohs and ahhs over the pie. "You shouldn't have, darling. Really, I said don't bring anything."

"It was the least I could do. I made it from scratch."

"I see that," Casey says. "Not for you, sweetie," she tells Ginger, who is jumping up to get a look. "This is for your mama. See what a nice pie the lady brought along for us?"

The dog is a handful, jumping up on the couch, then back down again for no reason at all. Sniffing Heike's bag, her feet and crotch. Barking. Trying to get up onto the counter.

"No, honey, you had your dinner. Now you come here and keep mama company."

Heike sits on the couch, next to Casey and Ginger, looking at the cartons of half-eaten donuts, the cans of dog food on the kitchen counter, the unwashed dishes. Clearly, Casey has reached the age where she's too old to be living alone. Heike can't remember whether she told her exactly how old she is. Eighty-five? Ninety? She looks older than Heike remembers. Heike remembers being impressed with how together she seemed when they met at the concert.

"Sit down," Casey says. "Make yourself comfortable. Can I get you something to eat?"

Heike is hungry, decides to say yes. What else can she do? She won't be able to sleep on an empty stomach. Casey seems delighted by this response. Tuna fish sandwich? Grilled cheese? Sardines on toast?

"Ginger's been nervous all day that you might not make it, but I told her don't you worry your little mind, my furry friend. Heidi is a good driver. She'll find her way." Heike, who thought she would have so much to say, isn't sure how to respond. Casey takes out a bowl of tuna fish from the fridge and prepares the sandwich, all the while telling Heike about Ginger's recent close call with the neighbor's dog, a pit bull Casey calls a bastard of an animal. "I'm gonna have to get me a shotgun and blow that sucker away if he doesn't leave my little girl alone," she says, giving Heike a fiendish grin.

Her hair is long and gray and uncombed, and Heike sees now what it is about Casey's smile that has been so disturbing: the woman is missing her lower teeth. *Pull yourself together*, Heike tells herself. *Al had false teeth. You'll probably also have dentures one day.* She begins eating the sandwich, sits with Casey on the couch, allows Ginger to do what she will.

Casey apologizes that she doesn't have a guest bedroom, tells Heike the couch is actually quite comfortable. "Sometimes I sleep out here myself. You help yourself to whatever you want from the fridge if you get hungry. Don't be bashful. Whatever you do though, just don't open the door if you hear someone knock."

"Someone knock?" Heike asks, still chewing.

"There's a man keeps coming by," Casey's says, lowering her voice. "He's crazy for me, but I told him: *I'm not interested.* I have my Ginger and that's all I need, but will he take no for an answer? Course not. He hounds me. That's why I had to get the chain."

Heike stares at her.

"Oh, he's not dangerous, honey. He won't hurt you. He's just love-struck, is all. He's love-struck for me, and he won't take no for an answer. Now I see I've got you all worried. You don't fret yourself over this. It's nothing, really. I just don't want him trying to snuggle up with me in bed is all," she says, grinning and patting Heike's leg with her hand.

Heike feels herself pull away. There's the smell again, inside her lungs. She finishes chewing, then excuses herself and goes to the bathroom. She doesn't have to use the toilet, but she needs a moment to sort out her thoughts. She's feeling disoriented. She can't remember why she decided to come up here.

As it turns out, the firmness of the couch isn't the issue. What keeps Heike from sleeping is the idea of spending three days with this woman. That and the stench. Not to mention Ginger's comings and goings. Casey told her, before turning out the lights, that Ginger would curl up with Casey in bed and sleep like a rock, but the fact is the dog doesn't sleep for a moment. Hour after hour she scurries back and forth from Casey's bedroom to the kitchen, sniffing and scratching and making a racket. At first she keeps coming over to visit Heike, trying to jump up onto the couch with her, licking her face. It isn't until Heike finally gives her a good smack that Ginger stays away.

Finally, impossibly, Heike falls asleep. She dreams something terrible. Someone is chasing her down a road. She's in her nightgown and doesn't have shoes. The road is foggy and there are headlights behind her, bearing down on her. Someone in a van trying to run her over.

A sound jolts her awake. She feels the trailer shudder as something crashes down above her, onto the roof. It sounds like a raccoon or possum, or maybe a skunk. It's still dark outside, and Heike can hear Casey snoring lightly. Heike goes over to the window and looks out onto the parking lot. There's a rusted wheelbarrow sitting up against Casey's mailbox, illuminated by a street lamp. Other than that and some old pickup trucks, she doesn't see anything. Whatever it was seems to have gone away.

Ginger is in the corner, by the TV, biting her hindquarters. She stops for a moment, looks at Heike, then gets back to business. Heike feels like she might cry. She's too old for this. She should be at home in her own bed, with her own pillow. She gets up to use the bathroom and then, instead of going back to the couch, she goes over to her things and quickly changes into the pants and turtleneck she wore on the drive up. The street lamp provides her with enough light to make sure she doesn't knock anything over. Ginger watches, keeping her distance. *Smart dog*, Heike thinks, as she zips up her bag and heads out the door.

No need to leave a note. Casey will figure it out.

Her body is exhausted, but adrenalin gives her a second wind. She gets in her car, puts the key in the ignition, and drives away. The clock reads 4:36.

She wonders whether she should drive to a hotel so she can get a decent night's sleep, then realizes she's actually less than two hours away from Seaside, the town on the coast where Galina lives. Maybe she'll drive over there and surprise her. Galina's place is big enough for Heike to spend a night or two. It isn't much, but it's better than Casey's trailer.

Galina might not be happy to have Heike show up unexpectedly, but what will she do—kick her own mother out onto the street? On Thanksgiving? Heike wishes she hadn't given the pie to Casey. It was right there on the counter by the couch. She could have taken it on her way out.

Who cares? Pie or no pie, Galina is her daughter. Amalia is her granddaughter. Didn't Heike send them a check for $200 just a few weeks ago to pay for Amalia's piano lessons?

Heike makes good time, driving from Paso Robles down to the 46, then over to Highway 1, where she begins to make her way up the coast. She'll be on her best behavior, won't ask for anything, will just sit there like a mouse. If Galina wants to let Amalia play with matches, Heike will watch while the child plays with matches. If Galina wants to keep the TV on all day and smoke in the house, so be it. If Adrian wants to drink beer out of the bottle and put his feet up on the coffee table with his shoes on, Heike won't say a word.

She'll just go with the flow. Whatever she does, she will not be pushy. She learned her lesson last time she visited—Galina made that clear, yelling at the top of her lungs, calling her a *controlling bitch*. "This is our house, Heike. Adrian is *my* husband. Amalia is *my* daughter. We call the shots here. Got it? I've dealt with your shit long enough."

Heike has developed a thick skin. She got over it. She forgave Galina. They are, after all, mother and daughter. Heike may not have given birth to Galina, but she brought her over here. Without her, Galina probably would have ended up as a beggar on the streets of Moscow.

The road by the ocean is often foggy this time of year. Heike takes the turns slowly, making sure to stay in her lane. The road is narrow. Occasionally a car comes at her from the opposite direction, but she manages to stay in control.

She thinks about the cute little outfit she bought Amalia last year for Christmas. She sent it up to Galina, along with a few other things. She didn't receive any photos of the girl—her granddaughter—in the outfit, but perhaps she'll wear it for Heike during this visit. She'd like that, to see the girl play in the red-and-blue outfit she bought for her.

She wonders whether Galina will make a nice turkey for dinner. A turkey with mashed potatoes and gravy and cranberry sauce. Maybe she's already up, making stuffing and putting the bird in the oven, the way Heike herself did all those years. Maybe Galina will offer her mother some sparkling cider. "We're so happy you could be here to celebrate Thanksgiving with us, Mom. You must be tired. Why don't you sit down and put your feet up? Rest for a while."

This is the thought Heike holds onto as the road curves and the fog lifts and she looks out into distance at the glorious blue sky. The sun is just coming up, and the world seems bright and full of promise and hope, like a painting. Heike doesn't feel worried as her car carries her toward that idyllic scene: the sky with a few perfect clouds in the distance, and the glorious cliffs, and below her the clear waters of the Pacific Ocean—the ocean Heike had wanted to visit so badly when she was a girl, halfway across the world in her tiny Bavarian village. Who would have thought that the girl whose mother woke her up one night, in the middle of her sleep, when the sirens were sounding, the girl who ran through the burning streets, holding her mother's hand, rushing toward the train station so that they could be among those lucky enough to scramble aboard the train as it was leaving the station, taking them away to the tiny village in the mountains that would become her home, the hut where she would live with her mother and brother for almost twelve years, who would have thought that girl would eventually have her dream—of seeing the Pacific Ocean and of making a life for herself in California—actually come true?

It's incredible how light the car feels now, how light everything feels. It's as if she were a girl again bouncing on her mother's knees. She sees Galina's face smiling at her. "Why don't you rest for a while, Mother. Sit down and put your feet up." She wonders whether Galina will bring her a cup of coffee. The sun is so bright. She can't really see, and suddenly she feels exhausted. Everything is catching up with her, and all she wants now is just to close her eyes and let go.

2013

Amalia

Two weeks ago, Adrian decided the agave had to go. From Galina's perspective, the cactus wasn't bothering anyone and actually made the place look a bit classier. "It's a nuisance," Adrian insisted. "It could put someone's eye out."

"I guess—assuming the person walked over to the thing and tried to French kiss it. Maybe then."

"There's liability issues, babe. We could get sued."

"Sued?" she said, putting a slice of the eleven-grain bread from the stand down the road in the toaster. "By whom?" She didn't know what had gotten into him. For eighteen months, ever since they'd moved into their tiny house just north of Big Sur, he'd never said anything about the agave, never mentioned its prickers and their attendant liability, never even touched the thing, but suddenly it was too close to the walkway that led from the carport to the front door. Suddenly it was a hazard, scheming to put someone's eye out.

"By anyone," he continued. "By the Adarkars, for one, if their kids play near it. Like if their ball comes over here."

"Okay, whatever," she said, getting out the jar of almond butter she bought to go with the bread. She unscrewed the lid and poured off the layer of oil that had accumulated at the surface, and, when she realized Adrian was putting on his jacket to go over and borrow the chainsaw *then*—not from the Adarkars but from their other neighbors—she decided she couldn't drop it. "You can't cut it down just like that, hon. Don't you think you should call Arthur? Don't you think you should at least ask his permission?" Arthur was their landlord, a doctor from L.A. who'd retired in Monterey, just down the coast.

"Arthur doesn't care what I do. You think Arthur wants that thing there? It's dangerous. What if we have a baby? What if the baby hurts himself?"

"Adrian, you're being crazy. You think a baby is going to jump up out of its crib and run over and fling itself onto a cactus? *It's a plant.* It's not hurting anyone. You're acting like it's a pit bull."

"I'm just saying."

Then, a few days ago, they were carrying in shopping bags from the grocery store, and—accidentally, on purpose—Adrian pricked himself on the arm. Either he wasn't watching where he was going or he went out of his way to jab himself, because there was no reason he should have hurt himself on the plant, but within thirty minutes there he was outside with the neighbor's chainsaw, going at the agave like a maniac. Galina tried to talk him down, to get him just to cut off some of the big stalks, the ones that were sticking out closest to the walkway, but who knows if he was even listening to her, he was so excited to have a reason to go all he-man.

So, in a way, when the agave sap got on his arms and made his skin feel like it had been lit on fire, it served him right. He came into the kitchen and wiped his arms with paper towels, but that only made it worse—spreading the toxic fluid on one's skin was not recommended. According to the Internet, you were supposed to wash the affected area immediately with soap and cold water. He ended up breaking out in a rash that he claimed was worse than being tortured in Abu Ghraib by that woman who blindfolded the Iraqi prisoners. For some reason, Adrian was obsessed with that woman and what she did to those guys. For months, he'd stood outside Albertsons with a petition.

Over the next few days, he used things from the cupboard that he insisted would resolve the hives covering his arms, namely vinegar compresses and baking soda. It wasn't until his skin looked like he'd contracted Ebola that he let Galina go and buy him calamine lotion and Burow's solution and something called silver sulfadiazine.

His arms were finally starting to look halfway normal again when the policeman came to their door. It was 6:45 A.M. on Thanksgiving Day, and Galina had just gotten up to make some Red Zinger. The sky wasn't really light yet, but they were in the habit of waking up early. Since moving in together, they'd fallen into a comfortable routine—tea in bed, followed by half an hour of quiet meditation, then fifteen minutes of chanting meditation. Afterwards, Adrian made steel-cut oats while Galina went to her studio to work on her sculptures. A woman in San Francisco had recently offered to give her a show.

"Sorry to bother you, ma'am," the cop said. He was big and beefy and looked like he might have once been attractive. "I'm looking for a Galina Silander."

Galina had never had anyone in a uniform come to her door before. Immediately, she wondered whether someone had found out about the weed she had growing in her studio. She wished she'd closed the shed door and locked it before she went to bed last night. She wondered whether Mrs. Adarkar had called in a complaint. "That's me. Can I help you?" The morning air was cold, and all she had on was her sweatshirt and a pair of Adrian's boxers.

"I have a woman in the car who says she's your mother. I found her on the road down south about fifteen miles, wandering around trying to get someone to stop. She ran her car off into a ditch, and, frankly, she's pretty lucky to be alive. Must be a tough old bird."

It took Galina a few seconds to process what the man was saying, to process the fact that her seventy-seven-year-old mother was sitting in the front seat of a cop car, crying, while she was fixing her hair with a brush that looked like it might have been used for one of her old dogs.

"I'm so sorry, Galina," Heike kept saying after Galina came down the driveway to see what the guy was talking about. "I told him not to bring me here so early. I didn't want to wake you up. Don't be mad. I told him we had to wait until nine. Are you angry with me? Please don't be angry."

"It's okay, Heike. I'm not angry." Galina gave her a hug, because what else could she do—and because Heike sort of collapsed in her arms, and kept crying and crying while the policeman stood by his car, playing with his phone and smoking a cigar. Eventually, Adrian came outside and gave Galina a look and then hugged Heike too. Heike hugged him back, tightly, and continued to sob.

It took quite some time to get her calmed down enough to explain what had happened. By then the cop had driven away, and Adrian had gone down to get Heike's car with the tow-truck guy, and they took her car to the only service station that was open, and Galina spent the morning with her mother reassuring her that, no, she wasn't angry, just concerned. "You could have killed yourself, Mom. Couldn't you have stayed in a motel or something and finished the drive once you rested? Couldn't you have called to let us know you were coming?"

"I wanted it to be a surprise. I thought maybe we could spend Thanksgiving together, as a family. I wanted to see Amalia. I haven't seen her since August."

For a while now, Galina had had some concerns about Heike's well-being, about the integrity of her mind, but this stuff about Amalia, this insistence on *seeing her granddaughter*, was the final nail in the proverbial coffin. This had been going on for several months now. Whenever Galina called Heike to check up on her, Heike would ask about Amalia, and Galina would have to explain that, no, she and Adrian didn't have a baby. They were still just thinking about whether they wanted to have kids. Occasionally, Heike would say something reasonable in response. "Oh, of course, darling. I'm so sorry. I don't know where I get these silly ideas. Of course you don't have a child yet." More often, however, she'd grow sullen and quiet and accuse Galina of trying to hide the girl from her, of keeping her away from her granddaughter to punish Heike.

This was the tack Heike took on this particular morning when she and Galina were sitting in the kitchen, Galina finishing her second cup of tea and Heike her third cup of coffee. "Heike, enough with the Amalia stuff, okay? There's no Amalia!" Galina snapped. Maybe it wasn't the best response, but even Krishna himself wouldn't have had the patience to put up with Heike for hours on end.

"What? Am I not good enough to spend time with the girl? I'm good enough to send money but not to see her in person? Is this how you treat me after I drive all the way up here to visit?"

Galina went back to her soothing voice. "You must be tired, Mom," she said. "Why don't you lie down for a few minutes and take a nap." Heike resisted at first, but eventually she let Galina lead her to the bed in the studio and help take her shoes and nylons off so she could get under the covers.

Now, nine days later, Galina is in Ventana Beach cleaning out Heike's house. Adrian has just left to go back to Seaside, and Heike is at the Saint Lucia Nursing Home, sharing a room with a woman from Reseda who had a stroke last year and hasn't been able to say anything since. Galina was surprised at how little fuss Heike put up when they told her they'd found a nice place for her to stay. At first it seemed as if Heike thought she was moving in with Galina and Adrian. She shifted in and out of lucidity. In the morning, she'd jabber on, quite coherently, about a show she'd just watched on TV or something she'd read in the paper, and then, like that, she'd accuse Galina of having taken her purse to get one of her credit cards. The crazy moments passed quickly, but it was impossible to tell what might trigger them. "Sometimes it's stress," one of the nurses said. "A change in routine. Even the weather can do it."

Whatever the case, Galina told herself that Heike was in good hands. Saint Lucia was clean. The staff came across as knowledgeable and patient, and, rather than alarmed at the change, Heike actually seemed happy to be around so many people. Right away, she took a liking to her roommate, a woman named Naomi, who, though she couldn't talk, smiled and nodded all the time, which, for Heike, was enough of a green light to sit next to her, chatting away endlessly.

Galina thought about calling Stewart right away to tell him about Heike's accident and the decision to find somewhere else for her to live, but she knew he didn't want to be involved in the details of Heike's unraveling. The few times Galina had tried to reach out to him over the years, he'd been rather curt with her, telling her he was busy working on his book. He'd always been a strange bird. "Uncomfortable in his own skin," was how Adrian described him.

And so Galina waited until two days ago, after Heike was settled into her new home, before she called Stewart and gave him the update. He seemed relieved to hear that Galina and Adrian didn't expect him to do anything. "What about money?" he asked. "I bet that place is expensive."

"It's all taken care of," Galina replied. "You know Heike, she's loaded. She gave me power of attorney a while ago, and I set up a monthly payment out of her account. Nothing to worry about." When Stewart realized Galina didn't want anything from him, he warmed up. He thanked Galina and asked whether there was anything he could do to help.

"Nope. Just sit tight. It's all under control." She didn't try to get him to visit Heike; she didn't bring up the fight that essentially ended his relationship with Heike six years ago. That was Stewart's business. Galina wasn't going to try to change Stewart. Everyone had to choose their own path. Her primary concern was packing up Heike's things and figuring out what she was going to do with Heike's house.

Luckily, Heike wasn't too much of a packrat. Galina and Adrian were able to sort through her things in just a few days, putting the clothes and plates and other kitchen things they thought Goodwill might want on the couch, and the stuff to be thrown out on the living room floor. Galina wasn't the sentimental type. She set aside a handful of keepsakes—photo albums, some of her mother's cheap jewelry—to take with her. Most of the stuff was junk, though: old cuckoo clocks that didn't work anymore, Christmas tree ornaments Heike had wrapped meticulously in tissue paper. Not surprisingly, the majority of the work involved sorting through Heike's papers—files about her various investments, old letters she'd saved. It wasn't until the third day after Adrian left that Galina came across a document related to her adoption: the letter from the orphanage in Lipetsk, in butchered English, describing Galina—"Girl, aged 5 years two months, blond hair, blue eye, above normal intelligent with deformity consisting of missing left arm."

There was no information to speak of about Galina's biological parents. On one of the forms, she saw the words "Reason for Abandonment"; in the adjacent space, there was a single word scrawled so quickly Galina couldn't make sense of it. When Galina was a girl, Heike had told her that her parents had been killed in a fire, but Galina had her doubts about that. If she'd been a different kind of person, she might have pressed Heike for more information; she might have tried to find the file she was looking at now. She might even have gone to Russia to visit the orphanage she lived in for the first five years of her life, to see whether she had any relatives in Moscow or Lipetsk or anywhere. But Galina didn't see the point in that. Her life was here now. For better or worse, her mother was Heike. Heike was about as messed up as they came, but she wasn't all bad. She'd seen a photo of Galina as a four-year-old girl, and she'd gotten on a plane and flown halfway around the world to pick her up and bring her back to the United States. She'd reached into her heart and taken pity on someone in need. She'd tried to do the best she could.

Until last year, Galina hadn't had much interest at all in being a mother herself. She'd gotten into her art—she was working on a series of collages featuring images of nude women from porn magazines from the '60s and '70s for a show in San Francisco—and between that and Adrian, she felt like her life was complete. The thought of having to wake up at all hours of the night to change a baby's diapers was not appealing. She had plenty of time for kids. Most people she knew didn't have kids until they were well into their thirties. Every time Galina told Adrian she didn't feel ready, though, he started singing the Billy Paul song "Let's Make a Baby." *Come on, come on. Let's make a baby. A little boy, a little girl. Girl, don't be shy, this is a moment we been waiting for.* Adrian had a really good voice, and he did a damn good impersonation of Billy Paul. For some reason, he was obsessed with having a big family.

Usually, Galina adopted a Western twang and told him to keep his belt buckled. A few months ago, though, something shifted for her. Maybe it was the fact that, squabbles aside, she felt happy with Adrian. Maybe it was the fact that she wanted to be the kind of parent she wished she'd had: someone centered and balanced. In high school, she was always angry at Heike. She always saw Heike as deficient—too needy, too self-involved, too narrow-minded. Recently, though, she's begun to see Heike differently, as a wounded soul, an unevolved spirit.

It's dark outside now. Galina is sitting in Heike's study, at the desk that used to belong to Al. She studies a photo of Al and Heike together in Hawaii, standing in front of a waterfall. And photos of Stewart in high school and college. And photos of Galina as a little kid and from her wedding. Galina isn't sure what to make of it all. In some ways, she feels no connection to these people whatsoever. But she realizes that, for better or worse, they are her family. Outside, she can see a tiny sliver of moon. It's the thinnest moon she's ever seen, so thin it looks like the eyelash of an enormous creature, an albino giant, perhaps, sleeping galaxies away. Tomorrow she'll drive back up to Seaside. She misses Adrian. She'll stop by Saint Lucia to say good-bye to Heike and drop off a few more things she thinks Heike might want—photos of Stewart and Gerry, and the ridiculous fur coat that Heike wears whenever she feels the least bit chilly. She's already put these things in the backseat of her car to make sure she won't forget them.

She goes to the living room and turns on the TV. She watches a rerun of *Law & Order*, then flips channels until she stumbles on *Singin' in the Rain*. At first she's not sure she's ever seen it before, but eventually, a few scenes come back to her—Debbie Reynolds popping out of the cake, the tongue twisters about *Moses supposes his toeses are roses.* Galina realizes that it was, bizarrely, one of the first movies she saw after she arrived in Ventana Beach. She remembers watching it with Heike and Al. They were sitting on the same couch she's sitting on now. She remembers laughing at the women in pink outfits singing in their strange fitted caps, and seeing Heike get up and pretend to tap dance when "Good Morning" came on. She remembers the dignified voice coach teaching the tone-deaf actress to soften her nasal vowels, and Gene Kelly singing "You Were Meant for Me" as he was falling in love with Debbie Reynolds on the empty soundstage.

It feels strange to watch the movie by herself now, alone in the house she grew up in. She considers the fact that this might be the last time she ever spends the night here. When the movie ends, she gets ready for bed. She puts on her sweatpants and a Patagonia top and goes into the bathroom to wash her face and brush her teeth. She keeps expecting to hear her mother's voice calling out to her—asking her to help get a box down from a cupboard, or find the checkbook she misplaced, or fasten a clasp—but the only sound she hears is the heat coming on periodically, that and the ticking of the clocks. The house feels larger without her mother's presence, larger and emptier.

2009

The
Sky
and the
Night

———————
■■■■■■

The dog's name was Marydog, named after the woman Ray loved, a dancer from Lubbock, Texas, who he swore was the most graceful creature he'd ever set eyes on. The Airedale was meant to lure the woman, his love, the angelic being he could not live without, back home: to coax her, if not to stay permanently, then at least to visit him for a time. The truth was that over the expanse of months and eventually years during which their romance had developed, he and his love had spent just a few weeks together—her arrivals always sudden, taking Ray by surprise, lifting the heavy fog from his soul until she disappeared again, equally unexpectedly, leaving him heartbroken.

Between visits, the woman, Mary Frances Lucero, a descendant, she claimed, of Spanish royalty, called from various payphones— motels by the side of the road, gas stations, truck stops—places that made Ray fear for her well-being.

"I love you," she said. "I miss you. I want to come home." This from a train station outside of Sacramento, California. "I'm having a baby, a baby girl."

It was his child, she said, conceived miraculously during a handful of rapturous nights, nights that still nourished him, the expression *miraculously* used by her and eventually him, because it was a kind of miracle that a woman who in four weeks would reach her fifty-ninth birthday and a man twelve years older could come together at this time in their lives and make love to the sound of ten thousand crickets lost in the high deserts of New Mexico and thereby create a new life.

Which is why, she insisted, she'd been compelled, months earlier, to get in her beat-up sedan, the car that broke down on the interstate 243 miles into her trip, and leave Ray in bed before the sun rose on a Tuesday morning in August—because she knew all she needed to know, that something was transpiring inside her body that required the attention of a medical professional, something that no one, not even Ray, could understand.

Ray willed himself to believe.

It was all that he had. His prior wives—the women from Germany and Hawaii and Florida and Japan—and his children and kinships had abandoned him decades ago, or he them; the result was the same: a house at the end of a gravel road twenty miles from town, a single dweller inside, a man with one set of clothes and three pairs of shoes, the soles of which he'd all worn down. His oldest son, the English professor, the one he held in highest esteem, hadn't called him in years.

The woman, Mary Frances Lucero, had smiled at him and filled him with hope. They'd met at a movie downtown, at the popcorn counter, where she spilled a bottle of Coke and he offered napkins to her. She was just passing through, visiting a show of some kind, a performance onstage whose details were blurred by her touch, for she had put her hand on his arm, in thanks and in gratitude for his napkins and succor.

Her touch filled his mind and his thoughts, and he wove a story from them. Perhaps they were both weavers of tales. Was she just a grifter bilking men out of money and hope?

She wore flowing clothes—loose dresses made of chenille and chambray, scented with elusive perfume. She drove out to his place, stayed with him, went away, and returned, always skittish and hard to pin down.

Ray pleaded with her to remain, cajoled and coerced, offered her bracelets and necklaces and tourmaline rings, but she had a mind of her own: she was a strong-willed creature, a woman who, once she set her sights on a course of action, could not be dissuaded. She would have the child, she insisted, their little girl, and she would raise it and care for it, whether or not her body provided the milk that it needed, no matter what Ray or anyone believed or said or countenanced.

What choice did Ray have but to wait? He sat at his table, looking at the crucifix on his living room wall—a figure of Jesus carved from cedar and painted by hand, the savior's arms stretched wide, a wreath of thorns on his head. Ray bought it in Mexico decades ago, along with a small wooden cross, from a priest who needed fast cash. He sold both items for a song, and Ray, who knew their true value, boxed them up carefully. The smaller cross was older by at least a century and was made of unpainted pine; it fit nicely in the palm of one's hand.

Outside, there was nothing but dust; the summers were dry, the arroyo parched with a paucity of rain.

The man, christened Raymond at birth, pictured her in her car, driving north and then west to a facility—in the heart of the Golden State's Central Valley, amidst farmland ripe with tomato and asparagus—that specialized in these kinds of things: unexpected pregnancies, complications from birth. A place with wide empty halls and fluorescent lights, with white curtains and machines designed to handle complexities of the female body. The doctors, the nurses, the orderlies, even the janitors that came in to clean had never seen anything like it, she said: a woman her age giving birth to a nine-pound baby girl, healthy as could be, right on schedule, graced with lungs as powerful as those of any child ever born in the state.

Against his better instincts, Ray willed himself to believe.

"You're a father," she told him from the hospital phone. "We have ourselves a baby girl." Name: Alma Lucero, after Mary's own mother and grandmother, a girl from a family of matriarchs, a girl destined, she declared, for a life full of promise. "She'll be a dancer, I'm sure," Ray's true love proclaimed. "She'll dance with the Bolshoi. She'll go to Moscow and Paris and Andalucía." All the places she, the woman, had always dreamed of visiting but had never been able to see.

There were of course details, issues to resolve, obstacles to be dealt with. How couldn't there be?

Ray waited patiently by the phone, willing it to ring, distraught when it didn't. He tidied the house, readying it for the woman's return, bought things for the girl, *his daughter*—things that rattled and made other sounds, colorful things, wrapped boxes, and yellow wallpaper. He made up a room especially for her.

On the one hand, he did these things; on the other, he worried. How was he, during the crepuscular years of his life, going to raise a little girl, should the woman, the ballerina, his one and only, come back and settle with him? There would be diapers and croup and other childhood ailments. Recitals and birthday parties. He readied the cupboards, swept the leaves from his porch. Two months later, he called a breeder he'd met in Los Alamos and bought the dog, an Airedale pup, the breed Mary Frances had said was her favorite.

From Sacramento, the woman traveled north, up Highway 99 through Yuba City and Live Oak, Chico and Los Molinos; she took the I-5 up to Redding, past the Whiskeytown National Recreation Area, eventually heading to Medford and Eugene and Salem. She had a friend in Salem, someone she'd performed with three decades earlier. She stopped at this woman's house—a nice place with a garden full of hydrangeas and rhododendron—then headed to St. Helens and Kalama, where again the car died, this time for good, on a road she referred to on the phone as Desecration Highway.

"What kind of horseshit name is that?" the man shouted back, standing in the kitchen in socks and a white undershirt. The phone had rung as he was getting dressed, and through the window above the sink he saw a crow looking at him. "Nobody in their right mind would name something Desecration Highway."

"*Desolation*," she said like a whisper. "It's just a two-lane thing," her words murky and garbled.

"I'm sorry. I didn't mean to raise my voice with you." But the line was already dead. He considered getting a map or maybe an atlas to determine whether there actually was a road with that name in the northwest portion of Oregon or near Tacoma. He thought about getting into his car and leaving the house, going in search of the places she claimed to have been, but what good would it do to separate fact from fiction, fancy from truth? Would it bring her home any faster?

That afternoon, he wired her money: money for the baby's food and a new stroller, for shots and medical visits. Then, six days later, money for bus fare from Portland, or Boise, or wherever she was, to Albuquerque, where he told her he'd be waiting at the Greyhound station with a bouquet of lilies and hyacinths.

"The baby has your eyes," she said, "red hair and eyes like a cornflower bouquet," and his heart did the thing it did when she used the voice reserved just for him.

"Her room is all ready," he said.

"Soon, Love. Just a little while longer."

"The dog misses you."

"Don't give up on me," she said. "I'm working at a motel down the road, the evening shift, to save up for the trip."

"*Money. Money.* How much more do you need?"

Then one day the phone didn't ring. Not that morning or the next.

Each day Ray got up and checked to make sure the dial tone was still there, brushed his teeth, turned on the TV, sliced bread from the loaf when it grew dark. "Don't worry," she'd said. "Soon enough I'll be home." He'd saved the message on the answering machine next to his bed. He listened to that, to her voice, to keep his spirits alive.

That autumn, as the sun began its slow descent in the west, Ray sat on the porch with the dog. "Soon your mistress will be home," he told his companion. And the dog, a good dog, a knowledge-able dog, a dog who'd grown up well, seemed to understand. He waited, but it was no use. A man can't survive on water and bread. A man can't eat a bit of salt and get through six thousand days. Each afternoon, he let Marydog out of the house so she could lie in the sun. He laid down a cushion filled with hay that she used as her bed, and sometimes he sat in the rocker and watched her rhythmic breathing.

One afternoon, the man went out to the portal to call her inside and saw she was no longer there. "Marydog," he hollered. "Time for your supper." He found her in the ravine, nosing around a pile of horse droppings and a rotten magpie. Two days later, he tracked her down in the apple orchard, mesmerized by a gopher's fresh hole. "You can't run off like that, girl," he scolded. "You scared me." But something had taken hold of her, something mysterious. Now when they went on their walks together, the dog ran off into the fields, deaf to the man's expletives and invective. At times, she didn't come back until the moon was high overhead.

The man himself took to wandering too. He walked for miles, in wind and rain, dry heat and hail, until his shoes were caked with mud, his socks and pants covered in foxtails, until the mountains in the distance grew dark and imposing. Until there was nothing but the sky and the night. He walked to the highway and watched cars passing by. He began to carry the wooden cross in his pocket, and sometimes he fingered it roughly, worrying the cracks of its surface. People came and they went, friends from the past, women he'd loved, especially the women, he thought. The women had always been hard to pin down.

Two summers and three winters later, when the man had let his beard and his nails grow long, when Marydog's coat had taken on the texture of something coarse and untamed, the phone rang.

It was her.

"I'm coming home," she said. He barely recognized the voice in his ear. He wondered whether it was an illusion, this thing—a phantom or ghost from the past.

"Meet me at the bus station. I've missed you."

Ray wept. He took the rugs outside to the porch and shook them until he was covered in dust. He rubbed mink oil on the dining room chairs. He got out a calendar and marked off the days.

It was a Tuesday, the day she said she'd return. He attached great significance to this fact. She'd left on a Tuesday and planned to return the same day. Something symmetrical cannot be undone, he reasoned aloud. He shaved off his beard and took a brush to Marydog's coat. He waited, willing the sun to rise and set, rise and set.

He washed his truck and drove into town, wearing clothes he hadn't worn in nearly a decade: a starched shirt and pressed slacks from the back of his closet. He bought flowers for the house. Gladiolus and marigolds and a dozen white lilies that had just started to bloom. He talked to storekeepers, telling them he was celebrating the return of someone he hadn't seen in, how long? He bought bags of fruit for the kitchen: oranges and persimmons, red and green grapes, tender fruit shaped like stars, things he imagined eating with her on the front porch. He arranged them artfully in earthenware bowls.

He bought chocolates from Europe, filled with marzipan and Swedish liqueurs.

The news didn't reach the man until three weeks later, seventeen days after the appointed morning came and went, four-hundred-plus hours after the bus pulled into the Greyhound station, bereft of her presence. "Sir," a female voice on the phone said, "are you a relation of Mary Lucero?"

At first the man thought it might be a joke of some kind, a prank by the woman herself, using an assumed intonation, an accent, because sometimes she played jokes on him, flirted using half-truths and narrative fabrications. "I'm afraid I have some bad news for you, sir. Ms. Lucero passed away a few weeks ago. She died peacefully, in her bed in the middle of the night. We had a funeral, a small gathering, just some folks here in the mobile home park."

Ray listened to her words, feeling the ground give way, pulling him into a sinkhole or an abyss.

"Sir, I'm terribly sorry. You okay, hon? Don't hang up on me now."

The man held the phone tight to his ear. Air caught in his lungs and parched throat; his body convulsed. He wailed, unable to contain himself any longer. He looked at the figure of Jesus, the crucifix mute against the cool stucco wall. He imagined dismembering the carving, splintering it into pieces, burning it in the arroyo with kindling from dead aspen and piñon.

"I'm so sorry," said the voice. "It's okay. You just go ahead and have yourself a good cry." Her name was Arlene. Arlene Reynolds, from Nashville, Tennessee.

The woman's name was Arlene.

Her skin was clear and unblemished, her hair long and thick, darker than Mary's, but attractive nonetheless. He found himself looking at her, this subsequent siren of his, fingering the snapshot he'd received in the mail: Arlene, who played in a bluegrass band once, long ago when she hoped she might become famous; Arlene, whose first husband drank half a bottle of whiskey a night and whose second husband, she told Ray on another long-distance call, died in an accident on the interstate just five miles from the trailer they'd bought near a 7-Eleven in Petaluma, California.

She had two dogs, two Pekingese—Maxy and Maxine, Maxy being the boy, Maxine the girl. "No, Mary hadn't ever spoken of any man out of state," Arlene said, "though she kept your number up on her fridge. That itself must have meant something. Mostly she kept to herself. I knew she was dating a guy who worked down at the lumberyard for a time, but I think she broke that off at least a year ago. Maybe more."

"I'm afraid I didn't see any children over there, no little girl."

Ray stood in the kitchen, looking out the window to his driveway, where a squirrel on a fallen branch was flicking its tail. The animal seemed alert to the world, almost flirtatious.

"She struck me as a nice person from what I knew of her. She sometimes brought Maxy and Maxine little snacks, Milk-Bones and such. When I had hip surgery two years ago, she brought over a few casseroles. Mostly, though, I think she stayed home with the shades drawn, watching TV."

Nine days after Easter, Marydog disappeared again. Increasingly, the man had taken to keeping her locked up inside the house, but, one day at dusk, when he was watering the aspen, she managed to sneak out. Ray set out a bowl of food and fresh water in case she returned. Each evening, he stood on the portal, calling to her. He looked up at the moon and listened to the coyotes. He wondered whether she'd fallen prey, seduced by their yelps and their cries. Three days later, in the morning, after a heavy rain, she appeared on the front porch, tail between her legs. "You scared me," he chided. "You shouldn't have run off like that." The dog cringed at the touch of his hand.

"No, I haven't ever been to New Mexico," Arlene said to him. Her pronunciation of the word *Mexico* intrigued him—in her mouth, the word sounded exotic, as if she had something wedged at the base of her tongue. He described the beauty of the desert for her: the color of the sky when the clouds broke after an afternoon rain, and at sunset, and at night, when the stars looked alive.

"I think you might like it here," he said.

"I'd need to bring Maxy and Maxine."

Arrangements were made; a new outfit purchased, this time by Arlene in anticipation of her upcoming trip. She had the car looked at to make sure it was ready. She hadn't expected something like this at this point in her life, she confessed.

A week later the man was down by the apple trees when he saw Marydog out in the distance. She turned and stared back at him. He called to her, but she didn't respond. He had a rope in the house that he'd bought at a hardware store, a rope the proprietor said could tame the most ornery soul.

"Here, girl," he called, holding out a delicacy between his thumb and forefinger. Sure enough, the dog came, head low, approaching him cautiously.

He fastened the rope to the trunk of a tree and then to the animal's neck, checking the knots to make sure she wouldn't break free. Afterwards, he walked back to the house, full of remorse. There's no other choice, he thought to himself. She's got a mind of her own. That night, as he lay in bed, the man heard the dog calling out.

The next morning, overcome with guilt and sadness, he washed out her bowls and gave her fresh water that was cool to the touch, and kibbles with chunks of cooked sausage. He saw she was up, standing on all fours. "I've brought you some breakfast, m'lady," he said, trying to smile, and as he approached, she growled, straining at the tether.

The man got a shovel and began digging the ground, the dog watching his every move. It wasn't a task he enjoyed. The sky was clear, and above the man, high in the sky, a single condor circled languidly.

Ray thought of Arlene. She's on the road now, he told himself. He wondered whether little Maxy and Maxine would like their new home. He wanted them to feel comfortable. He wondered what Arlene would be wearing—a yellow sundress, perhaps? He imagined her in high heels. Maybe she'd bring her guitar so they could sit outside on the porch, and she could sing to him. He'd always wanted to be with a woman who played guitar.

Arlene was a singer; he liked that. He looked forward to that.

He thought of the women he'd loved. The dancers and quilters and nurses who'd left him to fend for himself. He wondered where they were now.

The man's hands blistered, but he didn't stop. The hole grew deeper and, as he worked, he felt the sun on his back. He worked until he felt dizzy—from dehydration and exhaustion and the accumulated grief of his life. Finally, when the skin on his hands had begun to break open, he put the shovel down and wiped his brow. I'll sit for a moment and rest, he thought. He took off his shirt and looked into the brightness above. The sun was strong. Its warmth felt good on his face. He wondered whether he might see an angel, a spirit bringing comfort and grace. *Earth to earth, dust to dust,* he thought. It was a natural part of life's cycle.

He forced himself to keep his eyes open and not turn away. He wiped his brow, trying to make sense of it all.

Out with the old and in with new. Wasn't that the expression? It reminded him of a ditty he'd learned as a boy, and he smiled, not sure, now, how the tune went or even the words.

Hey, Diddle, Diddle—something, something—*three pigs with a fiddle.* It reminded him of being a sniffling runt of a youth, of going to the lake with his father and hunting for crayfish together. He remembered the metal pail he carried. He wondered what time it was and whether he'd have company soon, and he thought of all of the things that he needed to do between now and then. He put his hand of the nape of Marydog's neck and took hold of her tight, thinking of her and of Mary Frances, and of Arlene in the front seat of her car. He tried to picture her with her hands on the wheel, but his mind came up blank.

Life was uncertain, he'd learned, but at least his girl would stay. He took the wooden cross from his pocket and admired the single nail, the dark metal clasp, that held it together. The carving had been made quickly, it seemed, its edges unfinished. Ray pictured a man working alone by a fire, carving the cross's arms with a long weathered blade. He wondered what use the cross had served for the hunched figure. Had it brought the ancient soul luck? Had it served as a gift for the church? Perhaps the carver had given it to his wife as a talisman to ward off evil spirits or phantoms from other worlds.

Whatever the case, Ray had no use for the trinket, not at this point in time. It seemed fitting to him that he bequeath the curio to the dog, his erstwhile companion. Perhaps it would bring the creature luck as she made her way to Heaven or wherever it was she was headed.

If you are lucky in this life,
you will get to raise the spoon
of pristine, frosty ice cream
to the trusting creature mouth
of your old enemy

because the taste buds at least are not broken
because there is a bond between you
and sweet is sweet in any language.

—TONY HOAGLAND

2019

Buddy

Last night, after scouring the vegetable drawers in the fridge, Stewart set his alarm for 7:30 A.M. He set the backup travel alarm for 7:35, then brushed his teeth and checked both alarms again. Not that either alarm was actually necessary—he spent most of the night awake, dozing off briefly just after 1:15, then waking up for good at 2:54. He thought about taking a sleeping pill but worried that, even with the alarms, he might not get up in time. For the last twenty-four hours, his stomach has been going haywire, pitching and churning and making animal sounds.

Finally, at 6:45, he gets out of bed and makes a bowl of plain oatmeal. Maybe that will calm him down, he thinks, but when the phone rings at 7:50, he's managed to eat only a few bites. "Hello?" he answers. For some reason, there's a hopeful sound in his voice, though there's no reason to think it's Luis. Luis's plane won't arrive for another three hours.

"Hey, Buddy. Flight delay. American strikes again." The sound of Luis's voice still makes Stewart's adrenalin course. Luis says something else, but he's calling on his cell, and the connection is bad and the line goes dead.

Stewart finds the new arrival time online, takes a shower, and clips each of his nails meticulously. He shaves the stray hairs that have started to sprout from his shoulders, and then, before he puts on his underwear, he allows himself to look in the mirror, to examine the paunch that with each passing year grows more generous. At least he hasn't lost too much of his hair. He wonders how he will fill the day. He's already scrubbed the bathroom, done the laundry, swept the floors. If he were a normal person, he wouldn't be giving this visit a second thought. Twelve years ago, Luis moved to Austin, after dumping him. He's made it clear on numerous occasions that he has no interest in getting back together. He lives with a guy named Cramer now, someone who goes to the gym six times a week and likes karaoke. Someone who ran the Chicago Marathon.

Each December, Stewart receives a card with a photo of their Labradoodle, Bentley. Last year Bentley was wearing a Santa Claus hat. The holiday letter shared lots of good news—Luis's tenure at the University of Texas; the publication of his first book; Cramer's promotion at a company that makes online games, where he undoubtedly gets stock options and bonuses and generous raises. The letter included a few blurry photos of Luis and Cramer at Iguazu Falls and in Patagonia, where they'd gone on vacation. Stewart opened the card, read the letter, then went straight to his office and turned on the shredder.

Seven years ago, when Luis got back in touch with Stewart, he said he wanted to be friends. It had been thirty-four months since they'd seen each other, and Luis chastised Stewart for being petulant, for punishing him. Stewart tried to be mature. Of course they could be friends, he said, as nonchalantly as possible. Just one thing—could Luis please not call him *Buddy* anymore? It was the nickname they'd used for each other, and, Stewart said, the memories were too painful. Afterwards, he kicked himself for making such a big deal about the nickname thing. The fact is, however, that Luis agreed to Stewart's request. "No worries," he said. Luis doesn't call that often—once or twice a year, usually on Stewart's birthday, though this year he forgot that too—but sometimes when they're talking, Luis slips and uses the term of endearment. These days, the nickname doesn't make Stewart angry, just sad.

Twelve years is a long time. Long enough to get married, have kids, buy a house. In the last decade, people Stewart went to grad school with have published prize-winning books, received endowed chairs. Even Galina, the ne'er-do-well orphan who everyone thought would end up homeless, has managed to turn her life around—to get married and start a career as an artist. Last month she also called Stewart, out of the blue, and told him she was going to be in New York for the opening of a show. She asked whether she could come up and visit him on her way home. "I just want to reconnect," she said. "It's been a while." She stayed with him for two nights; it was the most time they'd spent together since she was in high school.

For a long time, Stewart blamed what happened with Luis on his mother. After all, it was Heike's conversation with Luis on the beach that precipitated his decision to move out.

"You treat her like shit," Luis said in the car after they left Heike's house in Ventana Beach. "She's really not that bad, Buddy." It was the Friday before Memorial Day, and they were driving up to San Francisco, but they still hadn't made it to San José. Traffic was backed up. They'd been planning to go to dinner with a friend of theirs who'd recently bought a postcard-perfect Victorian across from Golden Gate Park, and they were running late. They'd only stayed at Heike's place three nights, the first nights of the two-week trip they'd been looking forward to all year, but as far as Stewart was concerned, the vacation had been ruined.

Maybe Luis was right. Maybe Stewart was a misanthrope. Maybe he needed to lighten up.

The strange thing, the unexpected thing, was that Luis and Heike hit it off. After worrying for months that his mother would alienate Luis, Luis ended up liking her. He found her stories about the men she was dating hilarious. He thought her dirndl was a hoot. When she asked if he wanted to see Stewart's baby photos, he seemed genuinely interested. Stewart still remembers sitting on the couch, cringing, listening to his mother's stories about the apartment in Denver they moved into after his parents' divorce and how the Indian family next door kept making huge pots of vegetable curry and inviting them over for supper, how Heike taught their daughter to yodel. He remembers Heike cooking rouladen and dumplings and telling Luis about a man she met at the tennis courts who invited her back to his place for a Jacuzzi and what she referred to as a passionate lovemaking session.

Since they'd moved in together, three years earlier, Heike had harangued Stewart to introduce her to Luis. "Why not invite me out to Boston for Thanksgiving this year? I'm your family."

Or: "Bring him home for Christmas; we can all celebrate together. You'll have plenty of room. You can even have my bed."

Then: "Are you embarrassed by me? Is that it? Why keep me from meeting him?"

Finally Stewart relented. Luis had always wanted to drive up Highway 1, and they decided to fly to L.A. and make their way up the coast—stopping at Ventana Beach, then San Francisco, then Ukiah, where a friend of Luis's from college had bought thirty acres and built a two-room house without running water.

"Promise me you'll be on good behavior," Stewart implored his mother on the phone.

"Good behavior? What means good behavior? You're the one who gives me a hard time."

Maybe he shouldn't have threatened to cancel the visit. Maybe he shouldn't have made her swear she wouldn't throw any tantrums, that she'd allow Stewart and Luis to spend some time by themselves, that she wouldn't be needy and pushy and clingy. "You made your mom promise she wouldn't walk around the house in her bikini? You made her promise she wouldn't cry? Who does that?" Luis asked Stewart after they stopped at a gas station twenty miles north of her house. "You act like she's some kind of psycho."

In retrospect, what happened wasn't actually that big a surprise. Stewart had been planning to take Luis to the tide pools, and Heike asked if she could join them, and Stewart said no, she could not join them, because this was meant to be their vacation, an opportunity in their otherwise overscheduled lives for them to spend some time together alone, and could Heike please respect the fact that Stewart was an adult now and entitled to some privacy with his boyfriend? Despite Heike's promises that she would control herself, she started to cry and accuse Stewart of the usual litany of things, and then Luis intervened and said Heike was more than welcome to accompany them on their walk, in fact insisted on it, and Stewart, being perhaps a bit childish, told them they could go to the tide pools by themselves, because he was going to stay home and work on an article, and so Heike and Luis went off and didn't come back for three hours. What happened was Stewart's boyfriend and his mother hit it off fabulously, and Heike spilled her guts and told Luis how badly Stewart treated her, and how she wished she had a son like Luis, and Luis gave her a hug and calmed her down and ended up telling Stewart he needed to go back to therapy and work on his issues. What happened, after they left Ventana Beach, was Stewart and Luis had a huge fight, and Stewart flew back to Boston while Luis went up to Ukiah on his own, and when Luis returned to Boston, he packed up his things and said he thought they needed some time apart.

When Stewart finally gets in the car and drives to Logan, it looks like it might rain, maybe even snow. In ten days it will be Thanksgiving, then Christmas and New Year's. He finds it all dreadful. The holiday music, the candy canes in grocery store aisles, the fabricated excitement. For a while, after Luis moved back to Texas, people in Stewart's department took pity on him and invited him over to their homes for turkey and cranberry bread and stuffing and eggnog. It wasn't much, but it was something. Then the invitations tapered off until, eventually, they stopped altogether. Not that it really matters. In the end, when all is said and done, doesn't everyone end up alone?

Stewart wonders whether Luis still has his youthful demeanor. Well into his thirties, he could pass for a senior in college. At least Stewart isn't still living in the same apartment he and Luis shared. At least Stewart scraped enough money together to buy his own condo. And even if his career never took off the way he once hoped, at least he was promoted to full professor last fall.

When he gets to the terminal, Stewart finds the baggage claim and waits. He watches two bags on the carousel circle endlessly: a large black suitcase wrapped in tape and a smaller red bag covered with stickers of parrots. He wonders if the bags belong to the same passenger. Maybe the person never made it off the plane, he thinks. Perhaps the person got up in the middle of the flight to use the lavatory, and as he or she was sitting on the toilet, his or her heart decided to stop beating. Stewart imagines the body of a middle-aged man slumped over, pants down around his ankles. He imagines the stewardesses, in their dry-cleaned outfits, knocking on the flimsy door.

Sometimes, when Stewart is walking down the street, he senses that something terrible is about to happen. He imagines a truck swerving onto the sidewalk and plowing into him. Years ago, when he was still in therapy, his therapist asked how he felt when thoughts like this went through his head. She encouraged him to breathe deeply and visualize something peaceful and calm. Breathing deeply never helped. The thoughts didn't go away.

Watching the baggage carousel, Stewart breaks into a sweat. He takes off his jacket, then, moments later, considers getting up and going home. Luis might be irritated but he'd survive; he'd find a hotel—it wouldn't be that big a deal. Stewart weighs his options: wait until Luis arrives and pretend to be happy, make it seem like he's leading a balanced life full of friends and engaging activities and perpetual good cheer; or run out of the terminal like a maniac, screaming for help.

He tries to think clearly but can't. He imagines getting into his car and turning on the engine, sitting behind the steering wheel with his seat belt securely fastened around him as the car explodes. He imagines perplexed onlookers gathering around the flames. Before he can make a decision, he sees a stream of people coming down the escalator toward him—an African family in bright, patterned clothes; a large woman with ribbons in her hair, carrying a tennis racquet and a bouquet of flowers; a group of bearded backpackers who look like they've just returned from the Himalayas. Then he sees a man with a head of thick hair—dark hair, full lips.

Luis is wearing the same jacket he had when he lived in Boston, his hunter-green North Face parka. He smiles, gives Stewart a hug, tells him about his flight, about how much he hates traveling these days, how little legroom he had, how long he had to wait at the airport before the plane finally took off.

"What happened to Mr. Sunny Disposition?" Stewart asks.

"Mr. Sunny Disposition didn't want to come to this conference. Mr. Sunny Disposition wanted to stay home and go for a bike ride."

They walk to the car, Luis chatting about the classes he's teaching, about the fact that the paper he's giving at tomorrow's conference is a disaster, that the conclusion isn't even finished. Stewart wonders whether Luis will reach out and take his hand or his arm or brush some part of him.

Eight years ago, Stewart's father died. He had a heart attack while he was watching TV in his two-bedroom bungalow twenty miles south of Santa Fe. Four years later, Heike suffered an aneurysm. His parents are dead now. Stewart was estranged from them both, though he did make the trip out to California for Heike's funeral. His therapist told him to go, that it would give him the closure he needed. How many hours had they spent talking about his parents over the years? Hundreds? Thousands? If only Stewart had saved that money and invested in Amazon or Google or Netflix.

Heike's funeral was small—Bernie Kramer showed up, wearing of all things tennis shorts, and Crystal, who by this point had a family of her own, and Heike's current renter, a woman named Madeleine, a retired school teacher from Iowa who'd always dreamed of living in California. And, of course, Galina and Adrian, the eternally happy couple, the couple that could.

Frankly, Stewart was surprised anyone had shown up, given how much his mother had deteriorated. Before she died, an administrator from the nursing home had called both Galina and Stewart to tell them she didn't think Heike had long. Stewart thought about flying out to see her but decided it would be too painful. So many issues remained unresolved in their relationship. So many accusations and misunderstandings, so much ill will. He wasn't even sure Heike would have recognized him, the administrator having told him that Heike had become convinced Stewart had committed suicide. "These things happen," the woman said. "Sometimes patients who don't see their children for a long time think they've simply died. It's a way of coping."

The funeral took place on a hill overlooking the ocean, in the cemetery where Gerry was buried. Heike and Gerry had bought side-by-side plots. It was a beautiful day, and afterwards, Stewart went to lunch with Galina and Adrian. The next afternoon, he stopped by his mother's old condo. He knew that Madeleine had been close to Heike, that she'd visited his mother almost daily, and he wanted to thank her in person.

Madeleine invited him in for tea, told him to make himself comfortable on the couch while she got out some mint cookies she recently made. Stewart was surprised at how little the place had changed. The kitchen still had the same wallpaper—decorated with tiny roses and wheelbarrows—that he helped his mother put up when they lived there so long ago. From the couch, he told Madeleine that, when he was a young boy, he and his mother would sometimes eat breakfast on the porch overlooking the ocean.

"It's a wonderful view," she said, returning to the living room. "I can sit for hours looking out across the water. There's something so peaceful about it. Is it strange being back after so many years?"

"Strange?"

"I mean strange to be here now that your mother's passed away."

He reached for one of the cookies she'd brought out on a yellow ceramic plate, unsure how to respond. Afternoon sunlight filled the living room.

"It's not strange so much as bittersweet, I suppose. I have a lot of mixed feelings about the years we lived here."

"I know. Heike said you were quite an unhappy child. She said you hated living here." Madeleine had thick gray hair, almost like his mother's.

Her statement caught him off-guard. "I wouldn't say I hated it. It was perfectly fine."

"Maybe I misunderstood. Your mother always gave me the impression you despised this condo. Years ago, when I first got to know her, she insisted the minute she died, you'd put it on the market."

Madeleine's hands had a slight tremor, and he wondered how old she was. Late sixties? He wondered whether she herself had children. He wondered what else Heike had told her about him. Her impression of him was, he assumed, quite unfavorable.

"I assume that's why you're here, to give me notice. It's all right, I can vacate if that's what you want."

"Not at all. We haven't actually decided what we're going to do with the place. Who knows? Maybe I'll want to retire here myself one day." His words surprised him. He'd never actually thought about retiring in California.

"Well, it's a wonderful spot," she said and wiped her lips with a napkin.

It turned out they had quite a bit in common. Madeleine had lived in Boston for several years, before she met her husband and moved to Iowa. Like Stewart, she wrote poetry in her free time. Eventually, she asked whether he wanted to stay for dinner. "I have a chicken stew simmering in the crock pot. I can't eat it all myself." He hesitated, then accepted her invitation. Something about the condo felt cozy to him, and he had nothing else to do with his time, nothing pressing.

It wasn't until after dinner, as he was leaving, that Madeleine handed him the stack of letters, some in envelopes, others simply folded, page after page covered in his mother's handwriting. She gave him a hug and told him she was glad he'd taken the time to see her.

That night, Stewart and Luis go to a vegan restaurant Stewart has been wanting to try. There's a line of people waiting to be seated, and they huddle in the foyer next to a bulletin board covered with flyers advertising meditation classes and yoga retreats. Luis asks Stewart about his book on Allen Ginsberg, which he's been grappling with, on and off, for several years, and Stewart shakes his head. "Not that, Luis. Please don't ask me about the book; anything else."

"I hear you. Writing the paper for this conference made me want to puke. You'd think it would be easier to pump these things out the older you get, but, instead, it's getting so fucking hard. I have to bribe myself. You can't leave your desk until you've written two paragraphs; no lunch until you've written three hundred words."

"Three hundred words! Three hundred words would be huge. For me, a hundred words constitutes prolific output."

Stewart asks him what his talk is about. "You're going to love this," Luis says. "I went back to my dissertation and dredged up something from that." Luis's thesis was a comparison of Lorca and Neruda; he'd examined the ways in which the two poets had been influenced by Surrealism and the Modernist movements.

"Finally," Stewart says. "I never understood why you didn't do anything with it. I think you really had something solid." They talk about how hard it had been for Luis to finish his dissertation, how much he despised his advisor—a man from Chile who now ran a B&B in the Atacama Desert with a former student of his—until the hostess signals their table is ready, and they make their way past a man playing a kora to the back of the restaurant.

"I'm starving," Luis says as they sit down. "I think I'm going to start with the broccoli tofu, but you want to share a seaweed salad too?" Stewart hesitates. At that moment it feels as if they're boyfriends again. "I mean only if you want to. We don't have to."

"Sure, that sounds good. Let's get a seaweed salad. And maybe some edamame."

The tables are packed together and the place is loud, but the service is good. Within minutes they've ordered and Stewart finds himself asking Luis about his trip to South America.

"It was great. You have to go to Buenos Aires. It really does feel like Paris, and La Recoleta Cemetery is incredible." He tells Stewart about the Art Deco and Baroque mausoleums and the tombs of Silvina Ocampo and Adolfo Bioy Casares and Eva Perón. Luis is a talker, and he's several minutes into his description of the place he and Cramer stayed in Torres del Paine, when Stewart realizes he hasn't been paying attention to what Luis is saying. All night, he's been asking questions, one after another, about Austin's music scene and Cramer's job and Buenos Aires and Patagonia, but he's been having a hard time listening. He keeps wondering whether his breath is bad, and whether he should have gotten a haircut before Luis arrived, and whether he should have told Luis about his mother's death four years ago, when she passed away. He knows Luis is going to ask about her and that he will either have to lie—again—and say she's doing fine, or come clean with the truth.

"You okay, Buddy?" Luis says at one point, putting his hand on Stewart's knee. "What's going on with you? Here I am just yammering on." Stewart had prepared himself for this moment, actually planned what he would say when Luis finally turned the tables and asked him about himself. He decided he would tell Luis about a story he'd read recently by Alice Munro involving a woman with Alzheimer's whose husband takes her to a nursing home called Meadowlake. Stewart was going to tell Luis the story's plot: how the woman, Fiona, falls in love with another man at Meadowlake and forgets who her husband—Grant—is.

It was something he and Luis used to do when they lived together, recount stories they'd read to one another. Stewart took pride in his talent for retelling stories he liked, for being able to capture the writer's tone and narrative tension; Luis had said it was one of the things that had made him fall in love with Stewart.

"I read a story I think you would like," he planned to say. "It's about a married couple who've lived together for fifty years, who've spent their lives together, despite the fact that the man had an affair or two along the way. The man is a professor who's writing a study of Norse wolves, and like all relationships theirs has had its ups and downs, but part of the story's power is that you see the underlying commitment, the love between these two people, which, through everything—the man's affairs, the wife's failing memory—sustains them."

Stewart was going to tell Luis about Fiona's infatuation with the new man, Aubrey, and then he was going to ask: "Do you want to know how Grant responds? He doesn't stop visiting her, doesn't give up on her. He hangs on and keeps driving there, to Meadowlake, day after day, watches her play cards with her new crush, and whisper sweet nothings in his ear, and then, when Aubrey ends up leaving Meadowlake and goes home, do you know what Grant does? He sees how heartbroken Fiona is, and he drives to Aubrey's house and tries to convince Aubrey's wife—a real frump with a 'walnut-stain tan'—to let Aubrey visit Fiona again."

Stewart planned to pause here and then, after taking a sip of Armenian mint tea or whatever the flavor du jour was, he was going to look Luis in the face and say, "Imagine the commitment there: a man who would do that for a wife who's forgotten him completely."

Stewart hadn't decided whether he would quote any lines from the story—like the comparison of Marion to, of all things, a lychee nut (flesh with "oddly artificial allure . . . shallow over the extensive seed"). Nor had he decided whether he would tell Luis how the story ends (Fiona forgetting Aubrey and recognizing Grant again). The art of recounting a story derived, at least in part, of course, from the extemporaneous quality of the narration. It couldn't sound too rehearsed. And, in most instances, Stewart's narrations had always been improvised; there hadn't been ulterior motives.

Until now. Stewart wondered whether this time would be different, whether, like Scheherazade, he might use the narration as a tool. Was he really that pathetic? Did he actually think recounting Munro's story would soften Luis up, that he could use Fiona and Grant to segue into a confession about Heike's death, thereby playing on Luis's sympathy so that when they finally returned to his apartment Luis would have pity sex with him? Was that his plan? Had Stewart imagined they might actually end up falling asleep together—if not in each other's arms, then at least side by side?

Sitting across from Luis, picking at his Kuzu stew, Stewart realizes he doesn't have the wherewithal to pull it off. Instead, he says he's doing well, talks about a graduate seminar he's teaching on Flannery O'Connor, sidesteps Luis's questions about Heike. "She's hanging in there," he says. "I almost saw her last month. She was going to fly out here for an exhibit Galina just had."

"An exhibit?"

"Yeah, her art's really taking off. She had her own show at a gallery in New York."

"Seriously?"

"Seriously. She had a review in the *Times*. She's becoming a pretty big deal. She's doing these incredible sculptures made out of action figures and Barbie dolls. You know—like Thor and Batman and the Incredible Hulk. She pulls them apart and reassembles them in strange configurations so each one is a mutant, missing an arm or a leg or a head. Sometimes she makes prosthetic limbs out of sticks or pencils or pieces of metal. They're selling for $10,000 a pop."

"So you and Heike met in New York?"

"We were going to go. I mean I went down, but Heike couldn't. At the last minute she came down with the flu and decided to stay home." Stewart suddenly feels hot, feels another panic attack descending. He wonders whether he can excuse himself to step outside without having Luis figure out what's going on. He wishes he'd worn a short-sleeve shirt. So many restaurants in Boston turn the heat up too high in the winter. It's practically impossible to go out to eat these days, given how crowded things are, how noisy, and Stewart wishes he'd stayed home, had told Luis he wasn't feeling well, had never driven to the airport in the first place.

He knows he should *man up*, as his students would say—tell Luis the truth about Heike, because, after all, her death isn't his fault; he didn't *kill her*. He should tell Luis that he didn't actually go down to New York to see Galina's show, and that, yes, he does feel guilty, but he is after all human. He can't be expected to jump on a train at the drop of a hat just because someone has become *an artist*.

Luis reaches over and touches his arm. "Deep breath, Stewart. Have some water."

The next day, when Luis is at his conference, Stewart goes online and trolls various hookup sites. He navigates the ads with the dexterity that comes from experience. Two weeks ago he found an ad with a Ukrainian guy who'd just moved to Boston and needed a place to stay. The guy's photos were hot, and Stewart responded. The ad didn't promise sex in exchange for a place to stay, but that was clearly the implication. Stewart spent all afternoon cleaning the apartment, trimming his eyebrows and nose hair, bathing. He bought lilies for the dining room table.

Lilies.

But the guy looked nothing like his photos. He was at least fifteen years older and thirty pounds heavier, and his breath stank like sardines. Stewart let him spend the night on the couch but told him he had to leave in the morning.

Stewart promised himself that while Luis was at the conference, he'd work on his book, but here he is at 1:00 in the afternoon, in his pajamas, wasting the day. He's moved from his usual sites to his most recent discovery, a hustler site. He's only hired one guy so far, and that experience was such a disaster he vowed never to visit the site again, but he can't help himself. An hour later, the buzzer downstairs sounds, and Stewart lets in a guy who calls himself Vlad. Stewart's heart feels like it's going to split his ribcage wide open. He's beside himself with fear, with expectation and shame. He thought about hiding the knives in the freezer, but decided he doesn't care. If Vlad turns out to be a serial killer, so be it.

Miraculously, Vlad looks just like his photos. He looks better than his photos. He's twenty-three. He's visiting from Prague for eighteen days, and he's adorable—blond hair that's a bit too long, blue eyes. He has some acne and he's on the skinny side, but Stewart doesn't complain. He can't believe his luck. He offers Vlad a glass of water. They sit on the couch, awkwardly, and Vlad puts his hand on Stewart's leg. The entire encounter lasts forty-five minutes, at most. Stewart pays him, watches him dress.

"See ya," Vlad says as he grabs his Jansport backpack. Stewart gets up to open the door. He tries to give him a kiss on the lips, a good-bye kiss, but Vlad pulls away. "Not on the mouth," he says, angry. "I told you not on the mouth." Stewart closes the door and gets in the shower. He washes himself carefully. He examines his genitals, tells himself he's playing with fire.

He goes to his desk, turns on his computer, rereads the chapter he's working on—about *Kaddish*—which if one thinks about it, is quite fitting, given the circumstances in which he finds himself. He makes a few edits, then opens the drawer to his right and takes out the stack of letters Madeleine gave him when he visited her. He hasn't arranged the letters in a sequence meant to soften the emotional below. The first letter, the one he keeps on top, the one he's read so many times he's almost memorized it, is the one that makes him the saddest:

Mein lieber Sohn,

I have wanted to write you for such a long time, but I thought what is the point when there is no address for you. Sometimes when I take Summer to the beach I wonder whether you can see us walking together. Die Leute im Himmel schauen runter auf die Menschen auf Erden herab, *Omi always said to Dieter and me when we were still young. If you had learned German like I wanted you to, you would know what this means.*

Three days ago, I came across a box of your things in the garage. At the time when I went to your apartment to pack up your things, my feelings were still very raw. I could not read through all of these papers you had saved, but last night I took them out and looked through them again. I saw all of your compositions from college, where you got so many A's and the teachers wrote such nice things about you, and I found several photos you had saved in an album. It was quite sad to see the pictures that you had of us together from high school and during our ski trip to Mammoth. I always thought you had thrown these photos away, and I was happy to see that you had saved them. You even had the letter I wrote to you the night before you had moved away to college. It made me cry reading what I had written you once again.

How quickly times flies.

Do you know when I found out what you had done to yourself, I was actually quite angry with you? How could you not come home to pay me one final visit? There is so much we could have still done together. You had promised to go on a trip to Puerta Vallarta with me. Maybe traveling there would have cheered you up. Did you ever think about that?

The world is a beautiful place. Do you not miss it? Do you remember the last time we were together the hike we took up Rattlesnake Canyon with Roxy? Do you remember when you were in high school, the trip I took you on to Garmisch, how we hiked through the Alps, up to the Eibsee together? You always wanted to stop and decorate the cow pies with the Gänseblümchen and the raspberries we found. These are things I remember.

Sometimes I wonder what our lives would have been like if we had moved to Germany after your father divorced me. My German friends warned me against raising a child in the United States. Do you remember how close we were when you were young? Looking back, as much as I struggled, I think these were my happiest times.

I still remember how much we laughed when we drove to Dick Foster's house and put the pork chop and mashed potato dinner into his sheets. I wonder whatever became of this Lenora

Trinkhouse and her little Chihuahua. Do you remember this night and how much we laughed?

Perhaps if we had gone back to Garmisch we would not have grown apart. I always blamed the kids in school who were so mean to you for turning you against me. I know that they put so much pressure on you to always fit in. You wanted your O.P. shorts and Hang Ten shirts and I tried to comply but I knew it was just the beginning. Your father was no help whatsoever, with his latepayments and his pickiness which you inherited too. I know that I was not always able to give you everything that you wanted, but I tried to do what I could. I hope that you recognize this.

I wish so much you could tell me whether you are there, in Heaven, looking down from above in your white robe with oversized harp. It would make me so happy if you could come here to visit, even if just for a short time. Maybe the Angels will give you a guest pass to come down for vacation! Wouldn't that be something?? If so, I promise to let you eat the organic food that you like and don't make you eat any bacon or butter.

Love from your,
Mutti

Stewart is already in bed, reading, when he hears Luis return.

"Hey," Luis calls out. "Anyone home?"

"Yeah, hey," Stewart responds.

"Sorry I'm late. You know how these things are. Everyone wanted to go out for drinks afterwards, and I lost track of time."

"No worries," Stewart says. "Are you hungry? I made some chicken."

"Wow, thanks, I grabbed a bite on the way back though. I didn't know you were cooking."

Stewart tells him it's no big deal. "I'll eat it for lunch tomorrow."

"Did you see the moon tonight? It's a blood moon. It's pretty intense." Stewart shakes his head; he hasn't left the house all today. "It's pretty cool. It's like this orange UFO. You should take a look. These things only happen once every three decades."

Stewart takes off his reading glasses and gets out of bed. Does Luis really think he's going to get dressed and go outside to look at the moon? It's already 10:30. He's exhausted. He's pissed off. But he realizes this may be the last time he'll see Luis for a while. Luis's flight is leaving at 9:00 tomorrow morning, and his taxi is coming at 7:00. Stewart offered to drive him to the airport, but Luis told him not to be ridiculous. "I'm not going to make you get up at six on Sunday morning, Stewart. You've already gone above and beyond the call of duty."

Stewart shuffles out to the living room in his house shoes and asks Luis whether he has everything he needs. He stands next to the dining room table, watching Luis dig around in his suitcase.

"Hey, Buddy, I know it's late, but is it okay if I use your phone to give Cramer a quick call? I promised him I'd call tonight, but I forgot my charger."

"Sure thing."

Stewart waits a few more seconds, then realizes there's no point in staying in his living room, staring at Luis, like a dog hoping for scraps. "Help yourself to some cereal in the morning," he says, wondering whether Luis will come over and give him a hug. "I got Grape-Nuts. Is that still the kind you like?"

"Good memory! Thanks, but I'll probably just grab a muffin or something at the airport."

"Good seeing you, Luis," Stewart says, as he heads back to his room.

"Yeah, same here. Thanks again for letting me crash on the couch."

Stewart goes into his room and closes his door. He swallows a sleeping pill and gets out the earplugs he keeps in the drawer of his nightstand. He rolls them carefully between his thumb and forefinger to make sure they'll fit snugly. He wants to be certain that he won't hear Luis talking to Cramer. He doesn't want to hear Luis trying to be quiet, doesn't want to hear Luis laugh, doesn't want to hear Luis tell Cramer about his day. He doesn't want to hear Luis call Cramer *Honey* or *Soldier* or *Coco* or whatever nickname they use for each other. He wants to go to sleep.

He thinks about Vlad, about the way he closed his eyes just before he came. He thinks about his chest, hairless and smooth. Maybe Stewart will call him again. Why save his money? Maybe he'll invite Vlad to dinner. He wonders how much dinner would cost, how much Vlad would charge to spend the entire night.

I want you to pretend like we're boyfriends, Stewart imagines himself saying. Pretend you love me. Tie me up and spit in my face. He thinks about taking him to Iguazu Falls or on a cruise to Alaska. He's always wanted to go to Alaska.

Stewart likes the earplugs he uses. They create a barrier between him and the rest of the world. He feels the foam expand in his left ear, then his right. The sound of the outside world, of the radiator and the traffic and the creaking of the floorboards upstairs, slowly disappears. He feels like he's going underwater, like he's swimming down into the depths of a lake or the ocean. He hears nothing at all now. It feels like he's in outer space.

He's never believed in Heaven, though these days he wonders, occasionally, whether his mother was right and there is life after death—not with white robes and angels, but something. He wonders whether, perhaps, it is she who can look down at him from above or beyond and contemplate the person she brought into this world. If Heike can see him, he hopes she can't read his thoughts; he hopes what she sees is simply a man doing the best that he can.

Matthew Lansburgh
Outside Is the Ocean
Lisa Lenzo
Within the Lighted City
Kathryn Ma
*All That Work and Still
No Boys*
Renée Manfredi
Where Love Leaves Us
Susan Onthank Mates
The Good Doctor
John McNally
Troublemakers
Molly McNett
One Dog Happy
Tessa Mellas
Lungs Full of Noise
Kate Milliken
*If I'd Known You Were
Coming*
Kevin Moffett
Permanent Visitors
Lee B. Montgomery
Whose World Is This?
Rod Val Moore
Igloo among Palms
Lucia Nevai
Star Game
Thisbe Nissen
*Out of the Girls' Room and
into the Night*
Dan O'Brien
Eminent Domain
Philip F. O'Connor
*Old Morals, Small Continents,
Darker Times*
Robert Oldshue
November Storm
Sondra Spatt Olsen
Traps
Elizabeth Oness
Articles of Faith
Lon Otto
A Nest of Hooks

Natalie Petesch
*After the First Death There Is
No Other*
Marilène Phipps-Kettlewell
*The Company of Heaven:
Stories from Haiti*
Glen Pourciau
Invite
C. E. Poverman
The Black Velvet Girl
Michael Pritchett
The Venus Tree
Nancy Reisman
House Fires
Josh Rolnick
Pulp and Paper
Elizabeth Searle
My Body to You
Enid Shomer
Imaginary Men
Chad Simpson
Tell Everyone I Said Hi
Heather A. Slomski
*The Lovers Set Down Their
Spoons*
Marly Swick
A Hole in the Language
Barry Targan
*Harry Belten and the
Mendelssohn Violin Concerto*
Annabel Thomas
The Phototropic Woman
Jim Tomlinson
*Things Kept, Things Left
Behind*
Doug Trevor
*The Thin Tear in the Fabric
of Space*
Laura Valeri
The Kind of Things Saints Do
Anthony Varallo
This Day in History
Don Waters
Desert Gothic